PRISONER OF TIME

When Lucy Grantham chose to marry Reggie Denby, she little realized that the suitor she rejected, Bryce Fairfield, had decided to kill her. If he could not have Lucy, then no one would! Bryce, a brilliant scientist, planned no ordinary murder. His scheme involved luring the unsuspecting Lucy to his underground laboratory to exact his scientific vengeance. And here he encompassed not only his own doom, but also that of future generations as yet unborn!

JOHN RUSSELL FEARN

PRISONER OF TIME

Complete and Unabridged

LINFORD
Leicester

First published in Great Britain

First Linford Edition
published 2010

Copyright © 1952 by John Russell Fearn
Copyright © 2007 by Philip Harbottle

British Library CIP Data

Fearn, John Russell, *1908 – 1960.*
  Prisoner of time.- -(Linford mystery library)
  1. Rejection (Psychology)- -Fiction.
  2. Revenge- -Fiction. 3. Scientists- -Fiction.
  4. Suspense fiction. 5. Large type books.
  I. Title II. Series
  823.9'12–dc22

  ISBN 978–1–44480–029–6

Printed and bound in Great Britain by
T. J. International Ltd., Padstow, Cornwall

This book is printed on acid-free paper

1

Avenging entropy

The game of bridge had been a long one — and for one member of the company at least, a boring one. But now it was over. Two men stood in the cool of the summer evening thankful for escape from the warmth of the lounge. They smoked silently and disregarded each other until one of them spoke.

'Been a long evening,' Reggie Denby said, rather haltingly. 'Cards bore me — bridge especially so. Too much demand on the mind.'

'Yes,' the other said, noncommittally.

'Been worth it, though,' Reggie added. 'I'd sit through a thousand hands of bridge just to be near Lucy. S'pose you would, too?'

'One has to make concessions, even for Lucy.'

Silence again and more smoking. The

house at the back of the two men was not a big one but it was ablaze with light and the sound of voices. Nor was the garden in which they stood large. It was just one of those well-kept suburban patches shielded from the vulgar gaze by a high wooden fence upon which sprawled rambler roses.

The situation that existed now for the two men was not unique. They were waiting for Lucy Grantham to come out and reveal upon which of them she had decided. For months now each young man had ardently pressed his suit — Reggie Denby with the fervor of genuine love, and Bryce Fairfield, with the laconic brevity of a scientist. Bryce believed in himself and his capabilities as an electronic scientist: Reggie, having no such brilliance and existing merely as a none-too-bright salesman made up for the deficiency by being generous-natured towards everybody. Two men utterly apart in ideals and outlook, yet both centered on one young woman.

Then presently, Lucy Grantham came hurrying out to them. She was slim, in the early twenties, chestnut-haired and starry-eyed, at that time of her life when any young man would have been willing to confer his eternal devotion upon her.

'Sorry boys to put you through it with that bridge game,' she apologized, laughing, as she came up. 'But you know what dad is! Insists that bridge is the way to make friends.'

'Or enemies,' Bryce Fairfield murmured.

Lucy fell silent, studying each man in the reflected light from the house. There was Reggie — chubby, fair-haired, genial to the point of idiocy, his blue eyes fixed adoringly upon her; and then there was Bryce Fairfield, lean-jawed, sunken-eyed, with untidy hair sprawling across his broad forehead. He was unusually tall and always stooped. His flinty gray eyes analyzed everything upon which he gazed — even Lucy. Very rarely did he smile and certainly his associates had never heard him laugh.

'This, I suppose, is the hour of decision?' Lucy asked solemnly, fastening her hands behind her like a mischievous schoolgirl.

'If you wish to make it sound melodramatic, yes,' Bryce agreed. 'Frankly, m'dear, I don't see the reason for all these preliminaries — to say nothing of an evening wasted playing that damnable bridge. I could have spent my time to much more advantage down at the physics laboratory.'

'Oh, you and your chemistry — or whatever it is!' Lucy made a gesture. 'You keep your nose too close to the grindstone, Bryce. Anyway, you both asked for a definite answer, didn't you?'

'It didn't have to be a personal one,' Bryce replied. 'The mails are still functioning.'

Lucy looked astonished. 'Bryce, do you actually mean that my answer is of so little consequence it could have been sent through the *post*?'

'Your answer,' Bryce responded, 'means everything in the world to me, Lucy — but you know the kind of man I am. I cannot bear to waste time — playing bridge for instance.'

'Not even if it keeps you near me?'

Bryce was silent, his big, powerful mouth oddly twisted. Then the girl moved

4

her gaze from him across to Reggie. 'Reggie . . . '

'Yes, Lucy?' He moved with alacrity. 'Anything I can do for you?'

'I'll have plenty of time to tell you that later.' Lucy hesitated as Reggie absorbed the significance of what she was saying; then she turned to Bryce. 'Bryce, you do understand, don't you?' she asked earnestly. 'I think, now I've come to ponder it over, that there never was anybody else but Reggie.'

'From your attitude at times I hardly formed the same opinion,' Bryce answered. 'However, you've made the matter perfectly clear. You prefer Reggie — very well then. I am not the kind of man to argue over a fact. No scientist ever does. All I can do is offer my sincere congratulations to both of you.'

He caught at Lucy's hand and shook it firmly, so much so that she nearly winced. Then Reggie grinned dazedly as he found his own arm being pumped up and down vigorously.

'You — you know, I can't half believe it, Bryce! I never thought I stood a chance. You're so different to me — the masterful type. I thought that would impress Lucy quite a lot.'

'To every girl her choice,' Bryce said, shrugging; then in a suddenly more genial tone: 'I hope this is not going to interfere with our friendship, Lucy? I'd like to keep in touch, chiefly because I know so few women who'll take the trouble to be interested in me.'

'Why, of course!' Lucy laughed and patted his thin, muscular arms. 'You'll always be welcome, Bryce — always. What kind of a girl do you think I am?'

Bryce did not answer that. Instead he looked at her in a way she could not quite understand, his relentless gray eyes probing her. Vaguely she wondered what he was trying to analyze about her. He made no comment, however, and presently relaxed.

'Well, it's been an interesting evening, even if a disappointing one for me,' he commented. 'I don't see much point in staying any longer, Lucy. I'll go home I think and drown my sorrows in drink!'

'In physics more likely,' Lucy smiled.

'By tomorrow, Bryce, you'll have forgotten all about asking me to marry you. You're that kind of a fellow.'

'Mebbe,' he said, musing — but Lucy would probably have thought differently had she seen his expression when he arrived at his bachelor flat towards eleven that night. It was hard, the mouth drawn down at the corners, a light of vindictive cunning in the rapier eyes.

Without giving any heed to the necessity for sleep Bryce threw off his jacket, slipped on a dressing gown, and then made himself some coffee. Fifteen minutes after arriving in his flat he was in a deep armchair, black coffee at his side, and a stack of books within easy reach. Each book was an abstruse scientific treatise, but each treatise made sense to a mind like Bryce Fairfield's. His genius in matters scientific was far beyond the average. He would not have been staff-supervisor for the Electronics Bureau had it not been.

Chiefly, to judge from the notes he made and the books he studied, his interest seemed to lie in entropy and its effects. Not to any man did he breathe a

7

word of his private investigations into science's more mystical realms. To the staff at the Bureau — and also to Lucy and Reggie on those occasions when he joined them for an evening — he was still just taciturn Bryce Fairfield, making the best of having lost the girl he wanted.

* * *

For two years after their marriage Bryce remained an apparently firm friend of Lucy and Reggie, even to the extent of becoming godfather to their son Robert. In fact, it was surprising how much interest Bryce took in the family and their habits. In his brusque, matter-of-fact way he managed to find out everything they were doing, and knew of their plans for the future. Not that Lucy or Reggie minded. Bryce seemed to have become part of the family and he never once stepped beyond the bounds of friendship.

And, in the two years, his own fortunes seemed to take a decided turn for the better. From somewhere unknown he accumulated a vast amount of money, most of which he seemed to spend on scientific materials. He threw out vague hints concerning a machine he was building — and that was all. Then, one evening in the late summer, nearly two-and-a-half years after Lucy and Reggie had married matters swept up to a sudden and most unexpected climax.

The first sign came in an urgent 'phone-call to Lucy as she sat at home waiting for Reggie to return from a business trip down south. Immediately she went to the instrument in the hall and picked it up.

'Hello? Mrs. Denby speaking.'

'This is Bryce, Lucy. I'm speaking from a call-box near Little Oldfield. In case you don't know where it is it's some two miles outside Penarton where Reggie went on business today.'

'Oh?' Lucy was clearly mystified. 'But — but what — '

'I'm on my vacation at present,' Bryce hurried on. 'You remember me telling you it was about due? I'm taking it in the form of a walking tour. This morning, as I was on the tramp down south, who should pass me in his car but Reggie! Naturally I got in with him and most of the day I've stayed beside him, except when he's made his business calls. There's been a nasty accident,' Bryce continued. 'We ran into a telegraph pole through a fault in the car's steering-column. Reggie's pretty badly knocked about, though it's nothing serious. He's in the Little Oldfield Hospital down here. I sent for an ambulance and that's where they took him. I thought you ought to know right away.'

'You're sure he isn't badly hurt?' Lucy asked, her voice revealing her deep anxiety.

'Convinced of it. Best thing you can do is come down and see him for yourself — '

'I could ring up the hospital and . . . '

'That wouldn't help you to speak to him, though, would it? Never mind ringing up: just get down to Little Oldfield as fast as you can. By that time I'll have hired a car from the local garage with which to meet you. It won't take you more than an hour to get here. You take a Penarton train — they're pretty regular

— with a connection for Little Oldfield. How's that?'

'Yes. Yes, I'll start off right away. And thanks so much for helping me, Bryce.'

'That's all right. See you later.'

The line went dead. Lucy stood frowning, disturbed by the queer premonition that something was not 'quite right' somewhere. And yet — finally she turned to the directory, found the number of the Little Oldfield Hospital, and rang them up. There was apparently no mistake. Reginald Denby had been admitted that afternoon, suffering from abrasions and severe shock and his condition was unchanged.

Lucy wasted no more time. She set off for the station, leaving her mother in charge of little Robert, and as the evening was beginning to lower into darkness she found herself alighting at Little Oldfield Station, which was like an oasis on the edge of nowhere.

Outside the station Bryce Fairfield's tall, bony figure was visible, stalking around impatiently — then the moment the girl emerged from the station he came hurrying towards her, his lank hair disturbed by the restless wind.

'Good!' he exclaimed, putting a protective arm about her shoulders. 'You made it in good time, Lucy. Won't take me long to whisk you down to the hospital.'

'I hope he's no worse.' Lucy found herself propelled towards an obviously borrowed car. 'I rang up the hospital and they said there was no change.'

'He'll be all right,' Bryce assured her, settling down at the steering wheel. 'Nasty accident, but not serious. I wish to heaven it had happened nearer home and I could have had my own car at your disposal. This infernal thing came out of the Flood, I should think.'

Wheezing and protesting, it finally started up and Bryce drove it out of the station-approach onto a graveled road leading between dusty summer beeches. Lucy looked around her and frowned a little. The region seemed incredibly lonely and out of touch with the world.

'Terribly deserted spot, isn't it?' she asked, hardly able to suppress a little shiver. 'I just don't know this part at all.

Where exactly are we?'

'About fifteen miles from the south coast. We're in a region of old copper mines apparently: you can see the hills that have been created in boring them. Beyond those lies Little Oldfield itself. Won't take us long.'

Lucy became silent, again obsessed with that queer conviction that something was not 'quite right'. Bryce's expression certainly gave nothing away. His lean, saturnine face was without emotion as he drove the ancient car at its fastest, the summer wind setting the back hood flapping in dilapidated disorder in the rear.

It was not long before Bryce deserted the main road entirely and sent the car bumping and bounding along a rutted track, obviously long disused, leading between the somber hills of excavated earth from the mines.

'Bryce, are you sure you're going the right way?' Lucy turned to him in wonder after a while. 'There doesn't seem to be anything ahead but these copper mines — or what's left of them. If this is a short-cut . . . '

'I know what I'm doing!' he snapped, and drove on.

Lucy gave him another look of surprise, deepening to a growing fear. Then suddenly he pulled up sharply and pointed to a notice board. 'See that?' he demanded, and grinned harshly.

Lucy looked, but the board's inscription did not make sense to her. It said:

FAIRFIELD COPPER PROJECT —
KEEP OUT

Then, through her confusion, a light dawned.

'Oh, you mean this land belongs to you?'

'All of it!'

'And that's why you're using it as a short cut? It could not have happened better. Maybe we can get to the hospital all the quicker.'

'We're not going to the hospital, Lucy! Get out of the car!'

Lucy stared. Bryce repeated his command, with such fiendish determination that the girl did not dare hesitate any further. Bryce scrambled out after her and slammed the car door; then when he turned again Lucy noticed that he had an automatic in his hand.

'Just in case you get any funny ideas,' he explained. 'Now start walking and do just as I tell you — '

'Bryce, for heaven's sake! What's come over you? What about Reggie — ?'

'Be damned to Reggie! Carry on!'

Stumbling, terror-stricken, Lucy kept on going, satisfied now that her premonition of something peculiar had been justified. Not that it did her any good now: she was, she felt, at the mercy of a madman.

'Turn left!' Bryce commanded suddenly. She did so, finding herself following a hardly visible track, which led to the top of a mineshaft. Here a cage was standing as if in readiness. Was all this prepared then — she wondered? Evidently so, for she was roughly bundled into the cage and Bryce came and stood beside her. He had equipped the cage with some kind of electric device — not a difficult feat for a man of his scientific knowledge — the

15

flick of a switch setting the mechanism in action and plunging the cage into the depths of the long, disused shaft.

By this time Lucy's heart was pounding. Everywhere was pitch-darkness and she could hear the harsh, tense breathing of Bryce close beside her. His bony fingers gripped her arm so tightly she half cried out, then she was shoved forward brutally. The hand left her. There was a snap and light came up, filling a long tunnel with a dim glow. Along this Bryce forced her and at last into a well-lighted natural cavern.

Lucy came to a standstill, panting, her wide eyes looking around her. She paid no more attention to the steadily leveled gun in Bryce's hand. In every part of the cavern there seemed to loom scientific apparatus, none of it making sense to Lucy's completely unscientific mind.

'You needn't worry about Reggie,' Bryce said dryly, putting his gun away. 'They'll patch him up and turn him out when they're sick of him. Naturally, m'dear, the whole thing was deliberately arranged. I'd timed it in such a way that

16

that accident should have killed Reggie — only it didn't work out. Never mind; I'll correct the error later.'

'You'll — you'll what?' Lucy whispered in horror; then without waiting for an answer she hurried on: 'Where are we? What is this place? Does it belong to you?'

'Every bit of it, and all the land around it. First I made gold by synthesis of elements; then I sold it and made a fortune. I can have anything in the world I want — except you. And that's the part I don't like. I could have you, of course, but against your will. I don't want it that way. What I cannot forget is that you played around with my affections once, then kicked me out in favor of that idiot of a salesman! I've never forgotten that. I've schemed and plotted for this moment. I kept in touch with your movements. I knew I'd meet Reggie today because I knew just where he was going. I planned the accident that should have killed him and left me unhurt. I pushed him in the Little Oldfield Hospital in case you rang them up — '

'I did!' Lucy's eyes were bright with anger now.

'I guessed you might. But now you're here, m'dear, and you're going to be here a tremendously long time. So you turned me down in favor of Reggie Denby, did you?'

'I married Reggie because I really loved him, Bryce! I never could love you. You're too clever, too cold-blooded, too scientific — '

'I am going to show you, Lucy, what it means to turn me down,' Bryce interrupted deliberately. 'I made up my mind to do it on the night you chose Reggie.'

Lucy stared at him now with horror in her eyes, panic. She no longer had the courage to be angry. 'Bryce, you're mad!' she whispered.

'Perhaps I am — mad with jealousy.' He gave a shrug 'All I know is that if I can't have you then neither can Reggie have you any longer. You didn't like my science, you say? You will like it even less by the time I've finished with you!'

Suddenly he reached forward, clutched Lucy's arm, and sent her stumbling through a distant opening in the cavern into yet another lighted area. Lucy found herself again confronted by scientific machinery that she could not possibly understand. Fear, devastating enough to make her faint, surged over her as Bryce followed her in and locked the metal door behind him. Then he stood with his back to it, a ghastly smile on his lean face. 'This is one time m'dear, when you'll listen to science and listen well,' he said slowly. 'Take a look about you, at these tubes, these magnets, that table with the straps fastened to it.'

Lucy stared at the objects indicated as if mesmerized. Then she suddenly found her tongue again.

'Bryce you've got to let me out of here!' Her voice was a hoarse scream. 'You daren't do anything to me! You daren't! Reggie will find you and — '

'Reggie!' Bryce sneered. 'That moon-faced dolt? What do you imagine he could do to me? I'm one of the great scientists of this or any other age. No, m'dear, he'll do nothing. What is more, when I've finished with you I'll deal with him. Yes, him — and that squealing little brat to whom I was made godfather! I'll utterly destroy all three of you!'

As the girl stared at him hopelessly he continued: 'You have only yourself to blame, Lucy. You could have had me and all the power and wealth science can bring. You chose differently, and for that I have decided there must be a price.'

'Who are you to decide my life?' Lucy demanded frantically. Flinging herself forward she drove her small fists fiercely into Bryce's granite-like face, but he did not budge by a fraction. Finally he threw her away from him.

'Mad!' she repeated. 'Always an egomaniac, and now it has completely overwhelmed you! You're insane, Bryce! Insane!'

He remained motionless for a moment. Then he strode forward, gripped the girl in his powerful hands, and dumped her full-length on the steel table against which she had fallen. Before she realized what was happening the straps upon it were being buckled into place, across her neck, waist and ankles.

'Bryce, what are you going to do?' She

could hardly get out the words.

'Plenty!' He surveyed her pinioned form and smiled coldly. 'But first I have one or two things to tell you, things connected with the science you so obviously detest! You are going on a long journey, m'dear — a journey so long, indeed, that even I, a scientist, do not know where it will end. A journey into the future — alone!'

'What!' Lucy wriggled desperately in the straps, relaxed again, then breathed stormily. Her eyes fixed themselves on Bryce's merciless features.

'You, Lucy, are going to be the victim of entropy,' he explained. 'Naturally, you don't know what entropy is, do you?'

'You know I don't!' she shrieked. 'Let me go!'

'Entropy,' Bryce stated calmly, as though delivering a lecture, 'is the increasing disorder of the universe, the process by which the universe gradually moves to what is termed thermodynamic equilibrium. It can be likened to a perpetual shuffling, the disorder getting worse after each shuffle. Just like a pack of cards when we used to play that infernal game of bridge!'

'Bryce, for God's sake — '

'If only you had read Eddington whilst at school you might have learned something about entropy,' Bryce sighed. 'However, I've made it as clear as I can. Recently — ' his tone changed to grim menace — 'I fell to wondering what would happen if I created a non-entropy state, wherein nothing ever happens! So I decided to create a specified area — in this cavern to be precise — wherein molecular shuffling would achieve sudden and absolute equilibrium, a space wherein the ultimate of entropy would be reached instantly, instead of in a thousand, a million, ten million years' time. Do you understand that?'

Lucy was beyond answering.

'Yes!' he said, his voice harsh with triumph. 'I discovered how to create an entropy globe — a globe of force, the walls of which will attain absolute equilibrium, whose vibrations will extend inwards to everything inside the globe. Therefore, whatever is in the globe will be plunged into a state of non-time. Entropy will be halted! Progress will stop!'

'You,' Bryce continued deliberately, 'will be inside that globe, Lucy! At your feet is one magnet; at your head another. Between them they will build up the hemisphere of the entropy globe, and within it time for you will cease to be. You will be plunged into an eternal 'now' from which release may never come. If it does it will be at a far distant time when scientists as clever as I find the way to unlock your prison.'

'Bryce, I beg of you!' Lucy implored huskily. 'Let me go! I'll do anything you want. Anything! I'll divorce Reggie. You can't do this to me! I've so much to live for! My baby and his future! You can't do it!'

'On the wall there,' Bryce said, as though he had not even heard her, 'is a calendar, placed I hope so that you can see it. See the date? Seventeenth of August, two thousand and nine. Remember that well!'

'Bryce, you cannot — '

He flung a switch, keeping clear of the

23

steel table as he did so. Immediately an impalpable bubble of unknown forces — clearer than glass — enclosed the girl completely, swallowing up the steel table on which she lay. She was stopped in mid-motion of raising her head, her last sentence truncated.

Bryce waited for a moment or two, his brooding eyes on the many meters; then he turned and moved slowly towards the girl, contemplating her.

Her lips were slightly parted: her eyes stared at him quite unseeingly, eyes that were frozen and yet somehow alive.

His gaze went up and down her slim form in the light overcoat, which had fallen apart to reveal the brown silk dress beneath. Then he looked at the steel table, the four leather binding straps, and lastly the beechwood cradle supporting her shoulders.

Bryce smiled. Time, he knew, was no more inside that globe. Entropy was halted by reason of the globe's walls themselves having already achieved the ultimate of shuffling in their constitution.

'A year — fifty years — fifty centuries,'

Bryce murmured half aloud. 'Maybe for eternity.'

Then he turned back to the switchboard and examined the maze of instruments minutely. He waited perhaps half-an-hour and then cut the power out of the magnets at either end of the girl. A low, exultant sigh escaped him as he saw that the globe remained where it was, self-sustained, eternally balanced, a small foretaste of what the universe itself must one day become.

'If there is a key to open it — a random element to restore the shuffling — I do not know of it, nor do I want it! None shall unlock the prison!'

He nodded to himself, then pulling out a plunger he waited a moment and stepped back. In a sudden blaze of light and explosion the entire switchboard blew itself to atoms, tearing out part of the wall with it.

Bryce turned to the massive door of the cavern, took one last look at the motionless girl in the motionless globe. Then he closed the door upon her and locked it. With the face of a dead man he

25

went silently through the adjoining cavern and into the tunnel that led to the surface.

'Reggie and the brat,' he murmured, 'They must be taken care of too — '

The thought was dashed from his mind as there suddenly came a vast ominous rumbling. He looked up with a start, flashing the beam of his torch. He was in time to see the tunnel roof fissuring along its whole length. In a flash he realized what had occurred, remembering the crack in the cavern wall, which had followed the wrecking of the switchboard. The underground workings had been savagely shaken, and now — The truth had no sooner flashed across his mind than he saw a vast mass of rubble and stone hurtling down towards him.

2

Time barrier

The Master was deliberating. He sat in his office at the top of a building towering to two thousand feet — a lonely being with the entire Western world beneath him. His was the guiding brain, his the responsibility for the continued progress of western civilization. The people had voted him into his position, and his father before him. He knew only the duty and the inflexible adherence to laws made by his predecessors.

In appearance he was only slight. Like all his fellows he was deeply tanned. His movements were deliberate and every gesture had finality about it. His thin, high-cheek-boned face was without expression because he had been schooled in keeping his emotions in rigid check. In becoming more refined he had also become less human.

Presently the Master pressed a button amongst the multitude on his desk. Then he sat back to wait, the papers relevant to his next interview neatly arranged on the desk before him. A door with the warm gleam of copper about it opened and shut and a lithe, well-built man, scrupulously dressed and aged about forty, came forward with active strides.

'Good morning, Mister Hurst,' the Master greeted. 'Please be seated.'

'Master . . . ' Leslie Hurst gave a slight bow of acknowledgement and then settled in the chair at the opposite side of the Master's desk.

'I have here your dossier on the Eastern crisis,' the Master continued, motioning languidly to the papers. 'You apparently believe a good deal of trouble is brewing in that hemisphere?'

'I am convinced of it, Master — so much so I felt that, in my capacity as ambassador to the East, I should deliver that dossier to you personally and not risk the possibility of agents getting at it.'

'Very commendable, Mister Hurst. And what exactly is the Eastern position?'

'The same old trouble of concessions,' Hurst replied bitterly. 'Lan Ilof, President of the Eastern Government, is still insisting that half of Mars should belong to them and the other half to us. It's sheer bluff, of course, since we were the first to set up a base on Mars, and claim the entire planet for its value in mineral resources. Ilof claims that at a date before we arrived, their own expedition had already been there. He has supplied photographic proof to me, but I don't believe any of it. The whole thing boils down to him wanting half of Mars so that he can replenish certain mineral stocks of which the East is short.'

'And if he does not get this concession from us he threatens war?'

'Yes.' Leslie Hurst was silent for a moment or two, his young but powerful face troubled. 'And I think he could give us a run for our money too,' he added.

'How so?' There was an undisturbed calm upon the face of the Master that belied his quick-thinking brain.

'I happen to know that he has been building up formidable stocks of weapons and missiles with atomic warheads. Our agents have given me the facts. I don't think I would be exaggerating if I said his intercontinental missiles outnumber ours by nearly three to one. There are also many secret armaments. The scientists have never been deficient of scientific ingenuity as you know.'

'President Ilof has never seemed to me the kind of man who would favor war as a means of gaining his end,' the Master mused. 'I have met him several times, and I found him most cordial, and highly intelligent.'

'No doubt of it,' Hurst agreed, 'but he is in the unfortunate position of having to bow to certain factions in his government. Generals Zoam and Niol are, as is well known, two of the biggest warmongers ever. Their greatest ambition is to dominate Earth and now Mars. I know, because an ambassador hears many things. The Generals have never said as much openly, preferring to use President Ilof as their mouthpiece. That is the situation, Master,' Hurst finished. 'Nothing in the nature of an ultimatum has been presented yet, but I have the feeling it may happen before long. When it does I wish to be in a position to answer quickly, so what are your instructions?'

Calmly the Master answered: 'Tell them that we shall not make any concessions whatever. Not an inch! And if they wish to fight over it we will use every available means to defeat them. I am aware that it means war between hemispheres, global war on a far-reaching, devastating scale. Even that is better than meekly kneeling down before the dictates of a Government that has no legal right to make such a claim. Against the possibility of war breaking out I will instruct the necessary experts in the west to prepare armaments and defensive measures to meet the storm, should it come.'

'That is your final decision, Master?'

'It is. You may return to your post as ambassador, Mister Hurst, and any serious change in the situation must be notified immediately by secret transmission . . . A pity indeed that matters have to come to such a pass,' the Master added, musing. 'Particularly so as we are all now essentially a single race, the product of nearly one thousand years of world peace and inter-marriage — before the creation of a new iron curtain between hemispheres in the last century, for reasons that are now obscure.'

'Their comparative isolation in the last century seems to have bred a race of malcontents and warmongers,' Hurst commented.

The Master brooded, then said: 'Thank you, Ambassador Hurst. That will be all.'

Hurst rose, inclined his head, and took his departure. He had not been gone five minutes before the Master again pressed a button on his desk, and this time it was a thick-necked young man with broad shoulders, powerful hands, and a slightly intelligent forehead who came into the office. He had the easy stride of a man used to physical activity and, though well-dressed, gave the impression that he would have been happier in an open-necked shirt and working slacks.

'You have been trying to see me for some time, Mister Bradley,' the Master commented, eyeing him. 'I have admired your persistence, but not until now have I deemed it worth my while to grant you an interview. Take a seat.'

'Thank you, Master.' Clem Bradley sat down, his sharp gray eyes on the Master's tired, intellectual features.

'I understand,' the Master continued, 'that you are the technical chief of the Roton Gun Engineering Company?'

'That's right, Master. At the moment it is a very small company, I'm afraid, but at least I appreciate your kindness in granting me a license to get started.'

'That was not kindness, Mister Bradley. You were granted a license because it appeared to me, and my technical experts that you had developed a blast gun with significant possibilities. It would have been foolish to baulk you in your efforts to use this revolutionary gun. I am glad your little company is on its feet. What kind of contracts have you been getting?'

Clem shrugged. 'Oh, small ones. Doing a little mining in one place, blasting away ancient buildings in another. But we'll grow. I've got the business knowledge and my partner Buck Cardew is the right one to handle men. Between us we'll have a powerful company one day.'

'I am glad to hear it.' The Master consulted a file and then sat back in his chair. 'However, Mister Bradley, I did not of course summon you here to congratulate you upon your company. I am going to assign to you a project which calls exclusively for blasting equipment such as you possess.'

Clem's expression changed suddenly. 'You — you mean a Government contract, sir?'

'Obviously. I wonder if you recall, some little while ago, there being talk of a protective tower for this city in case of missile attack? You may remember that it was suggested we should have a mile-high tower, its summit equipped with every known radiation, the projectors emitting them to have universal movement to protect the city below on every side.'

'I remember it vaguely,' Clem admitted. 'It was not given a very big public airing.'

'For obvious reasons. The public at that

time would have reacted unfavorably to such an expenditure of money. Today, when hints keep leaking out of an impending crisis with the East, it is only sensible that we look to our defenses. So the Protection Tower — to give it its correct name — will come into being. The plans were drawn up long ago and I shall instruct the necessary engineers to go to work, immediately. Before they can do so the foundation shafts must be made, and for a tower a mile high they must of necessity be extremely deep.'

'You want the Roton Gun Company to drill them?' Clem asked eagerly.

'Exactly. The site we have selected, some fifteen miles from the southern coast, has a great deal of bedrock in it, chiefly to hold the tower foundations secure, and only the very finest blasting equipment will be able to make an impression. I am giving you the chance, Mister Bradley. When complete the tower will dominate the city at its southern end and also be the guardian of the sea as well. Now, here is the sketch plan of the foundation depth.'

Clem leaned forward, and from that moment onwards for the next half-hour he and the Master were in deep consultation. By the time he left Clem was not quite sure whether he was dreaming or not. A Government contract was the one thing needed to put any scientific business on its feet, and it seemed that the miracle had happened.

It definitely had, for the next day Clem, and his burly, iron-fisted partner Buck Cardew, transferred their men and equipment to the selected site fifteen miles from the south coast and began operations.

It was on the ninth day that they ran into difficulties, though when the morning shift began, there was no hint of trouble. Clem, looking about him on the surging activity deep below ground, mopped his face with his sweat-rag and settled his steel helmet more comfortably on his head.

'Another thousand feet ought to see this foundation space fully cleared,' he commented. 'We've been cutting clean since we started and the next push should finish it.'

Square-jawed Buck Cardew nodded. In appearance there was little to choose between him and Clem — except that Clem was obviously the man with the brains whereas, for handling gangs of men and moving equipment, there couldn't have been a better man anywhere than Buck Cardew.

'The Company's on its feet to stay,' Buck grinned. 'Thanks to the Master and his mile-high building — ' He broke off and released a throaty bellow. 'Hey there? What in hell are you boys wasting time about over there? Don't you realize we've got a deadline? Stop standing around and get on with the job.'

'Can't!' the ganger called back through his radiophone. 'There's a barrier here which even the blast-gun won't cut. Come and take a look.'

'He's crazy,' Clem growled. 'That gun of mine will blast anything in earth or space. Maybe they're just plain sick of groping around down here, and I wouldn't blame 'em. A surface demolition's much more interesting and healthy.'

'They're paid to work, and they will!'

37

Buck retorted. 'I'll soon settle 'em! Let's see what they're grousing about.'

Together he and Clem strode through the loose rubble of the floodlit space where the men were standing around the drilling apparatus. Buck put his hands on his hips and stared at the barrier facing the gun's blunted nozzle.

'Turn it on there!' he ordered.

A blasting, ear-shattering roar instantly followed, but that stream of livid, tearing energy which had been known to go through successive walls of steel, granite and diamond simply deflected itself in a coiling streamer of brilliant blue sparks.

'Kill it!' Clem yelled. 'What do you want to do? Blow us up with a backlash?'

Then as the commotion died down he clambered to the barrier and examined it carefully. It seemed to be dead black. 'Put out those lights!' he ordered.

The moment they went out and darkness descended it became clear that the barrier was not black but swarming with violet radiance. There seemed to be a multitude of pinpricks floating around in a vast bowl.

'What in blazes is it?' Buck Cardew demanded, as the lights returned.

'As a scientist,' Clem answered slowly, 'I'd say that it is force!'

'Huh? Force? But how did it get there?'

'Don't ask me. But I believe it is force built up into a resilient wall that simply deflects our gun-blast, much the same as the force-shields on our modern space-ships deflect meteorites. Looks as if we've run into something unusual. Have to weigh it up.'

Clem stepped back and started making a rough plan and sketch of the situation. Then, under his direction, prompted by Buck Cardew's bellowing voice, the gun was trained until it struck ordinary rock around the edge of the area. Gradually a way was cut round until the blue-black circle remained isolated.

Mystified, Clem and Buck clambered through into a deep cavern and stood staring in the light of their helmet lamps.

'Take a look at that!' Buck exclaimed suddenly, pointing.

Clem swung. Then his mouth opened in surprise as he found himself gazing through an impenetrable wall, which had deflected the force-gun. There was a girl visible, strapped to a table, her eyes staring unseeingly, her pretty face terrified.

'She isn't moving,' Buck whispered blankly. 'Say, she looks as if she's imprisoned inside a globe of force! Who on earth is she, anyway?' he went on in amazement. 'Look at her clothes! Girls haven't worn things like that for centuries!'

Clem's mind switched instantly to the scientific implications. He prowled around the cavern, examining it carefully, the astounded engineers piling in after him and dazedly contemplating the girl in the globe.

At last Clem halted, rubbing his jaw. 'Bits and pieces lying around suggest that this cavern was once a laboratory, but heaven knows how long ago. Even bits of iron and steel have rusted into ferrous oxide powder in the interval. Hundreds of years, maybe. What we've got to do is break down this globe of force somehow.'

'How?' Buck demanded. 'If a blast gun won't do it it's certain nothing else will.'

Clem thought for a moment, and then answered: 'If, as is probable, it was created artificially, it can be un-created.' He turned to the waiting men. 'Okay, boys, do your job. We've still a time-schedule to keep, remember. I'll use instruments on this and see what I can find out.'

The ganger nodded and blasting resumed, cutting a vast path at the back of the place. Clem gave quick instructions and had various instruments brought in to him. He figured steadily from their readings, quite oblivious to the shattering din and human shouts going on around him. After a while Buck came to his side, hands on hips.

'Well?' His keen eyes aimed eager questions. 'Any clues?'

'I think so, and most of them incredible.' Clem's voice had a touch of awe in it. 'It looks as though somebody way back in the past solved a scientific problem which still puzzles us even today. That globe, if the readings here are true, registers zero! It isn't there!'

'Are you crazy, or am I?' Buck

demanded. 'Of course it's there! We can see it!'

Clem motioned to the instruments. Sure enough they all registered zero. Clem gave a grim smile as he saw Buck rubbing the back of his beefy neck.

'I don't get it,' he said. 'And these instruments are the best that money can buy.'

'Surely. Nothing wrong with those.'

'Then what's the explanation?'

'It's something, as far as I can work out, that has no entropy. If that be so it means that it has reached absolute equilibrium. There is no interchange of energy to register. A little universe all on its own, which has achieved the state our own universe will one day attain. It is the same now, possibly, as when it came into being. For that very reason it is apart from all known forces. It is divorced from light, radiation, heat — everything. You see, it cannot assimilate anything more because it is assimilated to maximum. Nothing can go into the globe and nothing can come out of it.'

Buck was looking completely bewildered. 'Then how do we smash it up? Or open it?'

'Only one thing we can perhaps do, and that is warp it. Gravitation alone is independent of all other forces. Today we know that for certain. Gravity is a warp in the space-time continuum: it is not a force, as such. Down here we have gravitator-plates for shifting rocks. Maybe twin stresses brought to focus would warp this ball of absolute force and cause a rupture. Yes, it's worth trying!' Clem decided. 'This is quite the weirdest thing I ever struck.'

He gave further instructions and gravitator-screens of vast size were erected in the positions he directed. A past-master in stresses and strains, he knew just what he was doing, whether it would work on the globe or not was problematical.

It was an hour before he was satisfied, Buck Cardew becoming more and more impatient at such painstaking thoroughness; but at last Clem was satisfied and raised his hand in a signal. Simultaneously the power was switched on, a power exactly duplicating the etheric warp of gravitation itself. What happened then none of the men could afterwards clearly remember.

The globe burst with an explosion that hurled the engineers flat against the wall, pinning them there under an out-flowing wave of gigantic, hair-bristling force. The screens overturned and went crashing against the rocks. A rumble as of deep thunder rolled throughout the under-ground cavern and died away in the far distance.

Slowly the sense of released electrical tension began to subside, leaving the cavern heavy with the smell of ozone. Clem stood up gradually, turned, expecting to see the girl blasted to pieces. But instead she was definitely alive and wriggling to free herself!

' . . . do this to me!' she cried desperately, straining at the straps.

'Not only alive, but fighting mad,' Buck whispered, seizing Clem's arm and, staring at her. 'Why didn't she die when that thing blew up?'

'Because the force expanded outwards

from her. She was as safe as though in the epicenter of a cyclone.'

Clem strode forward and gazed at the girl's face. A most extraordinary expression came over her delicate features as she stared into the grimy visages under the steel helmets. Her dark-blue eyes widened in further alarm.

'What — Who are you?' she breathed weakly, going limp in the straps. 'Where's Bryce?'

'Bryce?' Clem gave her a baffled glance; then leaning forward he unbuckled the straps and raised the girl gently. He fished in his hip-pocket, spun the top from a flask with his teeth, then held the opening to the girl's lips. The fiery liquid, something she had never tasted before, went through her veins like liquid dynamite, setting her heart and nerves bounding with vigorous life.

Flushed, breathing hard, she looked in bewilderment at the puzzled men.

'Where's Bryce?' she demanded. 'Bryce Fairfield. He locked me in here with the threat that he was going after Reggie.'

'Oh?' Clem tried not to look too vague.

'Matter of fact, miss, I've never heard of Bryce — nor Reggie. That reminds me!' Clem broke off. 'When you recovered a moment ago you said something. What was it?'

'I said: 'Bryce, you can't do this to me!' '

Clem shook his head. 'No! You only said: 'do this to me!' There was no beginning to your sentence. I noticed at the time that it sounded odd. I assume this Bryce Fairfield was in here when you started your sentence?'

'Yes — yes, of course he was. He was going to throw a power-switch which would have . . . ' Lucy's voice trailed off as she gazed around the cavern and at the unfamiliar blasting equipment. 'Everything's different,' she faltered. 'There's no switchboard now, and no door . . . Tell me, who are you?'

When none of the men answered Lucy's gaze swung to the calendar, or at least to the place where it should have been. There was only a mass of crumpled rock. She gave a gasp.

'There was a calendar there!' she cried.

'It said seventeenth of August, two thousand and nine. Where's it gone?'

'Two thousand and nine!' Buck Cardew exclaimed. 'Hell! No wonder you're dressed in such old-fashioned clothes!'

'Old-fashioned?' Lucy's voice caught a little as she looked down at herself. 'But how can they be? It's still two thousand and nine, isn't it?'

Nobody answered. Grim looks passed between the men.

'Well, isn't it?' she cried, nearly in tears; then Clem put a gentle arm about her shoulders.

'Better hang on to yourself, miss,' he said gravely. 'This is the year 3004 A.D.'

All trace of colour drained from the girl's face. She half tried to smile and then went serious again. She was obviously utterly stunned.

'3004,' she repeated. 'That's nearly a thousand years. It can't be true! It just can't!'

'I'm afraid it is,' Clem said, his voice quiet as he saw her distress. 'We can't even begin to understand the situation or try to help you until we hear your side of the story. Who are you? What happened in this cavern?'

'I'm Lucy Denby and — ' Slowly the girl unfolded the story. The men listened in grim silence, looking at each other when it was over.

'I wish I could have had a few moments with that Bryce Fairfield,' Buck murmured, clenching his fists. 'I'd have hit him so hard they'd have had to scrape him from the wall.'

'A thousand years!' Lucy repeated again. 'I just don't understand it! What am I to do? Do you realize what has really happened to me?'

'You felt nothing during this enormous lapse of time?' Clem asked thoughtfully.

'Nothing whatever. Except that I seem to remember I felt a passing wave of dizziness when Bryce threw in the switches. Even then I hardly realized what he had done. I couldn't see anything clearly through the bubble wall. Then, in what seemed a matter of seconds — certainly no longer — you appeared. So now,' Lucy finished hopelessly, 'I'm utterly alone. My husband long since dead, and my baby too, assuming that he ever grew up.'

'Unfortunately,' Clem said, 'we can't put back the clock. All we can do is offer you the hospitality of this day and age.' He rubbed his jaw and then gave an uneasy glance. 'At least, I hope we can offer you our hospitality,' he amended. 'You see, things have changed a lot whilst you have been a prisoner. Today everybody is tabulated and indexed, and you're a sort of odd girl out. If your lack of an index-card is discovered you may be executed.'

'Executed!' Lucy stared in horrified amazement.

'Anybody without an index-card, without even a proven line of descent, is deemed outcast by the Government Council or else the Master himself, and promptly eliminated. In that way spying and sabotage is crushed. We shall have to be extremely careful how we handle things. What makes it doubly difficult is that a new war is threatening.'

'There is still threat of war?' Lucy asked hopelessly. 'There was a similar state of affairs when in my own time, various countries were at loggerheads with each other — '

'Long forgotten,' Clem interrupted. 'Today the trouble is between hemispheres. This is the West against the East: something to do with planetary concessions. But it's war just the same, and that being so, your position is awkward.'

'Surely I will be allowed to explain the situation? Or you can?'

'Not on the basis of what I know so far,' Clem answered, sighing. 'I don't even begin to understand the genius of Bryce Fairfield. I'll have to work out exactly what he did and then submit my findings to the Master. Once he is satisfied — and there is no guarantee that he will be — you will get city status and become one of us. But in the meantime — '

'There's my wife,' Buck Cardew interrupted. 'She was to have Worker Ten to assist her in house duties. I could arrange it so that Worker Ten is bought off and Mrs. Denby here takes her place. It's been done before and could be done again. How about it?'

'Risky, but maybe worth it,' Clem answered. 'We'll do that; then I can keep in touch with you,' he added, looking at Lucy. 'For the moment you had better stay here with us and then come along home after dark. We'll look after you — and you'll have an awful lot to see,' he finished. 'Things have changed enormously since your day.'

'I can imagine,' Lucy said, and gave her first faint smile.

At about this time, in the wilderness of the city's huge powerhouse, Chief Engineer Collins studied the peculiarity with cold blue eyes. For the first time in his thirty years' supervision of this master power station something was wrong. The smooth night-and-day rhythm of the giant engines, which fed a city sprawling over nearly every part of what had once been the British Isles, fostered and tended by complicated robots, was being interrupted. There was a very slight flaw in the uptake of power. Perhaps it was only carbon dust. It had happened once before, twenty years earlier.

Collins summoned testing-robots. They

came up with their many instruments and gathered about him, obeying all the commands he planted in their reasoning brainpans. With mathematical exactitude, far keener than even his excellent reasoning, they traced the flaw and handed out the report.

'Intermission fault of one ten-thousandth of a second,' Collins mused. 'Bad! Definitely bad!'

Turning, he slammed in switches and was immediately connected with the slave powerhouses in other parts of the city.

'What's your power report?' he questioned.

It was given him immediately. There was nothing wrong there, but there was here, and what was more it was becoming worse. The sweetly-humming giant had taken on a definite lobbing sound, like the thud of a flat tire on a smooth road.

Struck with the unbelievable thought that there might be a flaw in the metal, Collins turned to the gigantic balance wheel, which formed the basis of the master-engine. He had just reached it when something happened.

A pear-shaped swelling appeared suddenly on the edge of the mighty wheel, only visible as a mist with the wheel's rotation. It grew at phenomenal speed — and then exploded! Flung by centrifugal force, mighty pieces of metal flashed to all parts of the powerhouse. One struck Collins clean on the forehead and dropped him dead where he stood. The robots looked on impartially, their guiding genius lying mangled on the floor.

Immediately the other engines ceased to work as an automatic contact breaker clamped down on the entire area. The alarms rang. The emergency bulb went up on the desk of the chief powerhouse controller at City Center.

Breakdown, for the first time in thirty years! It was incredible.

3

Bridge of death

Clem Bradley, Buck and Lucy Denby, were in Clem's little autobus doing two hundred miles an hour down the traffic-way bridge to City Center when the power failed. All of a sudden the vast, long line of light and steel that had held the girl in thrall went into total darkness.

'What the hell — !'

Clem let out a gasp of amazement, then his hands quickly tightened on the switches. Never in his experience had he come up against a sudden blackout like this. It was utterly unheard of. He slammed on the emergency brake, but either he slammed too hard or the steel was faulty, for the pedal snapped clean off under the pressure.

He was too astounded, too desperately busy, to exclaim about it. Like a madman he tried to cut down the power of the engine as the autobus raced onwards into the unrelieved darkness, the bridge girders, faintly visible against the sky, whipping past at dizzying speed.

'Hey, stop this thing!' Buck Cardew yelled. 'There may be something ahead, and if there is, at this speed, it'll be the finish. Where's your search-lamp?'

'Switch it on for me,' Clem panted. 'I've all I can handle!'

Throughout this hair-raising performance Lucy sat in frozen alarm, the wind rushing past her face as Buck fumbled on the control panel. Then suddenly the blinding cold-light brilliance split the darkness ahead.

'Look!' Lucy cried hoarsely.

But Clem had already seen it — the unbelievable — a vast fissure glowing mysteriously across the traffic-way itself. The bridge was breaking in two! There could be no other explanation. And below there was a drop of a quarter-of-a-mile into the brimming waters of a river.

'Jump it!' Buck yelled. 'Full belt! You'll just make it!'

The why and wherefore flashed

unanswered in Clem's brain. He gave the autobus everything it had got, shot over the crumbling edge of the fissure, then slammed with shattering force onto the other side of the bridge. So terrific was the shock that the front wheel axle snapped like a carrot, slewed the car round, and then — plastered it with splintering impact against the cross-girders at the bridge side.

'Whew!' Buck whistled in relief, mopping his face. 'That was too close for comfort. You okay, Miss Ancient History?'

He heaved the slumped girl up beside him and she gave a nervous little laugh. 'Yes — yes, I'm all right, but — ' She stared at the waters so far below and wondered if the river might actually be Old Father Thames still on his way to the sea; then she twisted her head to survey the still enlarging gap in the bridge. 'Just what is wrong?' she asked finally.

'Hanged if I know,' Clem snapped. 'First my brake pedal broke off like a matchstick, then the front axle gave way, and the bridge is rapidly — '

He broke off and stared as headlights

flashed into view on the distant dark stretch.

'They'll go over!' he gasped, vaulting over the car's side. 'Maybe I can warn them in time.'

He went pelting back along the bridge, pulling out the safety red light he used underground and flashing it as he ran. Desperately he waved it to and fro. He saw, as the first vehicle came hurtling nearer, that it was a public service transport. Closer — closer, until he could read its brightly illuminated number-plate — KT 897.

'Stop!' he screamed helplessly. 'Stop, you fool!'

The driver saw the danger too late. The transport went plunging over the edge of the broken bridge, a private autobus behind it following suit. Dazed with horror Clem watched both vehicles go hurtling down into the wastes below. The cries of the doomed people floated up in a ghastly echo.

'My God,' he whispered. 'All those folks — '

'I can't get the emergency station,'

Buck said, hurrying up. 'If the bridge is cracked then the wires along it will be too.' He stopped, his eyes widening as he stared at the fissure. 'Look at the infernal thing, Clem! It's still enlarging — !'

'I know.' Clem's voice was grim as he shifted his gaze from the depths below. 'There's something incredibly wrong about all this, Buck. First the light and power goes off, and then this — '

'Altogether,' Lucy remarked, not finding it easy to keep a hint of sarcasm from her voice, 'my arrival in a time a thousand years ahead of my own hasn't been too auspicious.'

'Believe me, Ancient, things like this never happened before,' Buck insisted.

'Confound it, Buck, the lady has a name,' Clem objected, but the girl only laughed.

'I rather like being called 'Ancient'. It's so different. And it sounds natural coming from you, Buck.'

Buck scratched the back of his thick neck as he tried to determine whether Lucy was serious or not; then Clem spoke again, obviously preoccupied with the problem on hand.

'It's incredible that tried and tested steel, rustproof and everything, should start behaving in this way! Forgetting the brake and axle on the autobus for a moment, take the case of this bridge. For a hundred years it has been regularly overhauled. Supersonic testers have proved it to be absolutely perfect without even an air bubble or inner fault. Yet now it behaves as though suffering from atomic blight — '

'What's that?' Lucy enquired curiously.

'Oh, a sort of corrosion which afflicts metals if they have been in contact with atomic radiation anywhere. But in the case of this bridge such a thought isn't even admissible. No; it's something else, but don't ask me what.'

'Something coming up from the distance,' Buck remarked. 'It looks like an emergency car.'

He was right. In a few moments an emergency official transport came speeding up from behind them. A uniformed officer jumped out and came hurrying forward.

'What's gone wrong here?' he demanded, and Buck promptly gave the details whilst the official glanced around him, taking in the situation. Finally he turned to his driver.

'Send a radio call and have the bridge closed at both ends pending examination. Had a smash, eh?' he went on, surveying the shattered autobus.

'Just leapt the gap in time,' Clem answered.

'I don't understand this at all,' the officer continued, frowning. 'This steel here is like treacle, just melting away. I hear the same sort of thing happened in the master powerhouse this evening. Flywheel went spongy, or something, and just blew to bits.'

'Oh?' Clem looked thoughtful. 'It did, did it? Any serious damage?'

'Chief engineer killed and light and power cut off. It's the impossibility of it all. This city is so flawless the thought of even a screw coming loose is unheard of. Anyhow, let's have your index-cards.'

Buck delayed in handing his over whilst Clem did some fast thinking to explain away the anxious Lucy. Presently the officer turned to her and she looked at him uneasily, fumbling in the borrowed mining tunic which Clem had loaned her before they had left the site.

'Come along, miss!' the officer insisted impatiently. 'I have a lot to do.'

'S-sorry. I — er — I seem to have lost my card.'

'Of course you did!' Clem exclaimed suddenly, trying to sound as though he had just remembered something. 'Don't you remember, when we were out of town something fell and we were in too much of a hurry to bother with it? That must have been what it was.'

'What's your number?' the guard asked.

'She's Worker Ten, Domestic Section,' Clem said quickly.

'Domestic Section? What's she doing out here, coming from the city outskirts?'

'She was staying with friends and we picked her up,' Buck Cardew said levelly.

'Mmm, I see. See you produce your index-card at Civic Headquarters tomorrow, without fail.' The officer handed Lucy a ticket. 'Now all three of you had better get off this bridge. What's left of your car will be returned to you later on. Move along, please.'

They turned away, glancing at each other in the dim light.

'That,' Buck commented, 'was even more uncomfortably close than that dash across the bridge. We'll square it all right tomorrow with Worker Ten's card.'

'Uh-huh,' Clem agreed absently.

'Queer,' Lucy remarked, 'that a bridge of steel should actually melt like that — and a powerhouse flywheel fly apart and a brake snap on the car. Sounds very much like 'troubles never come singly' as we used to say in my time . . . ' Her voice trailed off into wistfulness for a moment; then it dawned on the two silently pacing men that she was crying softly to herself.

'Here now, Ancient, this won't do,' Buck told her, his great arm about her shoulder. 'What's wrong? Homesick?'

'Wouldn't you be?' she asked, between sniffs. 'There's Reggie, and my baby, and — It all seems so recent to me. As though only a few hours ago I was with them. And now I'm here, with the knowledge that I can never see or know of them again.'

'It's tough all right,' Clem agreed, dislodging Buck's arm and putting his own in its place, 'but we'll look after you. We're not such bad folks when you get to understand our ways — even though we'll probably seem a bit regimented.'

More pacing and Lucy slowly recovered again. Then she asked a question: 'I suppose you've no idea what's gone wrong with the steel?'

'None whatever,' Clem replied. 'It's a complete mystery.'

'I've got one angle on it,' Buck said, thinking. 'It's probably the work of Eastern agents. They're everywhere, honeycombing the West. Some new scientific devilry of theirs, I'll gamble.'

'Possibly,' Clem agreed. 'If so, they've got a mighty fine weapon!'

They finished the rest of the journey on foot, each busily thinking, and by the time they had reached Buck Cardew's home in the city's heart, the lights had come on again and power was working normally.

Mrs. Cardew, slim, practical, and

dark-headed, was clearly discomfited by the power failure.

'Is something the matter, Eva?' Buck asked in surprise. 'Outside of the blackout, I mean.'

'Yes, Buck, I — ' She stopped, looking past Clem towards Lucy.

'Friend of mine,' Clem smiled. 'Lucy Denby. We found her in rather peculiar circumstances — well, we'll need you to help us.'

'I know you can,' Buck added reassuringly. 'This girl has got to have protection and she can't get it anywhere better than right here.'

'Willingly,' Eva assented. 'But who is she? I mean what Grade?'

'No Grade at all. She's come direct from 2009 A.D. She's an Ancient Briton. Remember reading about them in the History Recorders?'

Eva Cardew stared blankly; and she stared even more as the story was unfolded to her. Finally she looked at Lucy for confirmation.

'Yes, it's true,' Lucy sighed. 'I'll try not to seem too dense in face of the scientific wonders you must have in this Age of yours, and I do thank all of you for the way in which you've helped me — '

'Buck,' Eva interrupted, 'we can't get away with this! I didn't know this girl was not registered. It's a risk we can't afford to take! Don't you realize that if we're caught sheltering her, and she has no index-card to produce, we can be lethalized?'

'Course I know,' Buck growled. 'What about it? You don't suggest we turn the poor girl loose, do you? Anyway, that's all sorted out. I'm canceling Worker Ten, and Ancient here can take her place.'

'That,' Eva said, 'will be more difficult than you think. Worker Ten was killed tonight on an in-town transport. It went over the bridge on which you had such a narrow escape.'

Clem started and Buck's eyes widened.

'Was it Transport KT-eight-nine-seven?' Clem questioned sharply.

'It was. They gave it out on the local newsflash not ten minutes before you arrived. That was why I was looking so bothered when you came — trying to decide about my household duties.'

'This,' Buck groaned, 'is the finish! The authorities know that Worker Ten is dead, along with hundreds of other people, and we told that officer that Ancient here is Worker Ten.'

'Yes,' Clem muttered, 'we did.'

Silence, Lucy looking from one to the other uneasily.

'So there it is,' Eva said, glancing at her. 'You can surely see, Lucy — I suppose I can call you that — that we can't jeopardize our lives by having you stay with us?'

'And what's the alternative?' Buck asked. 'We can't turn her loose in a city and time she doesn't know anything about. It would be worse than murder! And certainly Clem can't take her to his place since he's known to live alone.'

'Suppose we got married?' Lucy asked surprisingly.

'Huh?' Clem stared at her, uncomprehending.

'I mean it,' she said. 'I'd trust you anywhere, Clem — or you, Buck. You're both grand fellows. Don't you see?' she

66

went on eagerly. 'If we got married, Clem — in name only of course, since I'd be doing it solely to protect myself — we could live together in safety and decency, and then Buck and Eva wouldn't have anything to worry about.'

'Now I know you're an Ancient Briton,' Buck smiled. 'Do you mean that in your time marriages were entered into as lightly as that?'

'Sometimes, yes. Just get a special license, a Justice of the Peace and the thing's as good as done.'

'Not any more,' Clem said, with a serious shake of his head. 'If we tried to get married, Lucy — and don't think I don't appreciate the compliment — we'd be worse in the soup than we are now. First your index-card would be needed; then you would have to go before the Eugenics Council for a medical examination. Then I would have to do likewise. After a gap of about six months the Council would decide if we were fitted to marry each other. If so, special forms would be granted, fully indexed mind you, and then a rubber stamp would proclaim us mated. Not married: that word is defunct. Marriage today is a biological partnership of ideally suited male and female parties. So say the great ones.'

'Then one doesn't marry for love any more?' Lucy asked in amazement.

'Sometimes it works out that love and eugenics match. In the great majority of cases you only get biological matches. Good idea in some ways. It has stamped out disease, the unfit, and the over or under-prolific. No, Lucy, that wouldn't do.'

'She stays here!' Buck declared flatly. 'That was the idea in the first place, and it still holds good. Tomorrow, if we haven't thought of anything bright, we'll smuggle her to the underground site until we do think of something bright. Nobody from the law will get down there without your express permission, Clem.'

'Looks like the only solution,' Clem admitted. 'Think you can fall in with our views, Eva, and take a gamble?'

'I wouldn't want you to,' Lucy exclaimed. 'It isn't fair that you should be asked to take such a chance. I'm all for giving myself up to the authorities and explaining the facts.'

'They'd listen, no doubt of that,' Clem said. 'If they didn't I think I could get the Master to give us a hearing — and his word is law. But unless I could prove what we were saying I'd get nowhere. And there isn't a shred of evidence!'

'Not even in these ancient clothes I'm wearing?' Lucy pulled aside the overalls. 'Ancient to you, that is.'

'Not even those. You could have obtained them from the history museum — or, if none have been reported missing from there, you could have manufactured them on a synthetic clothing machine. Most women have them these days.'

'Then — then what about these biological experts you have?' Lucy hurried on. 'Surely, if I submitted to an examination, they could find things different in my make-up to those of a woman normal to this time? In a thousand years there must have been some sort of evolution.'

'Not in a thousand years,' Clem replied

seriously. 'It takes tens of thousands to alter a physical characteristic so far as to make it noticeable. You think back to your own time, and then to people existing a thousand years before you. How much change is there to be detected?'

Lucy sighed. 'None. To the eye, anyway. Even two thousand years doesn't seem to make much difference. I never thought we could be so stumped for proof. The force-bubble gone, the cavern blown up, and all traces of Bryce's handiwork rusted into dust.'

'That brings us back to my own idea,' Buck insisted. 'No other way, Ancient. You can see that too, Eva, surely?'

Eva seemed to have made up her mind — or else her overbearingly generous husband had made it up for her. She turned to Lucy, smiled, and then said quietly:

'All right, Lucy, I'll risk it — ' and to cement the fact she shook hands warmly. Then she began to move into action. 'Take off those overalls and make yourself at home. I'll fix an extra place for you at the table. You'll certainly be in need of a meal?'

'Starving,' Lucy confirmed, struggling out of the overalls with Clem's help. When at last she was free he patted her shoulder.

'Everything will be all right,' he assured her, smiling seriously. 'I'll be along tomorrow with some plan worked out. Meantime I can rely on Buck to keep you hidden if anything unpleasant arises.'

'You're not staying for a meal?' Buck asked.

'No, old man. Better get back for when that wreck of an autobus is returned to me.'

With that Clem took his departure. Lucy, whilst Buck departed to other regions presumably to freshen up, found herself surveying more closely this typical city home of the year 3004. Basically she could see little difference from the more modern homes of her own time, but here and there were refinements that fascinated her. The wall, for instance, facing the warmly-glowing electrode fireplace was composed of two panels. In one was inset a flat television screen; and in the other a loudspeaker permanently on by law so that any official notice could not fail to be received.

Another refinement was lack of corners. The room was almost circular, floored in a rubber substance of scrupulous cleanness, and all the furniture was metal. The two doors leading off the room slid on runners instead of moving back and forth. Fascinated, Lucy began to wander to the nearer doorway and found herself looking in on the kitchen where Eva was busily at work.

Everything was electrical, and thermostatically controlled, dials and meters in the walls ensuring exact temperatures for cooking and culinary necessities. At the moment Eva was in the midst of operating a highly-polished and complicated-looking machine. 'Come in,' she invited, noticing Lucy watching.

Lucy did so, surveying curiously. Apparently there was no necessity to handle anything. From the washing-up machine to the robot dish-cleaner everything was automatic.

'What are you doing?' Lucy asked curiously.

'Preparing an extra meal for you. All you do is put the concentrates in this funnel here and then they drop inside this machine and all sorts of queer things happen. Don't ask me what because I'm no scientist. The finished result is a perfectly cooked meal. That is if you don't object to a beef omelette?'

'Object? I'd love it.'

Lucy glanced up as Buck came into view again. He was in shirt and trousers, his skin bright red from a vigorous washing, and in one hand he was clutching his pants' belt. 'Something wrong here, Eva,' he said. 'Maybe you can fix it for me. My belt's given way.'

'Given way?' Eva looked surprised. 'But that's the one I bought you for your birthday. Ox-hide. It couldn't give way.'

Holding his trousers with one hand Buck handed the belt across — or at least the two halves of it. It had parted down the centre back as though it had gone rotten.

'Nice thing!' Eva exclaimed indignantly. 'I'll take it back to the store tomorrow! I've been swindled.'

'Looks like it.' Buck drew in his pants' waist by another notch and then rubbed his hands. 'Well, what about the meal, sweetheart? I'm starving.'

'Coming right up. I'll just get Lucy some more suitable up-to-date clothes first. She can borrow some of mine; we're about the same size.'

Lucy did not say anything but thought a good deal. In a thousand years home life had changed but little, she decided. Only the externals were different. It brought back to her vivid memories of her own life with Reggie, and once again she felt like crying. Somehow, though, she kept a hold on herself, and after quickly changing into the borrowed clothes Lucy gave her — Eva taking away her old ones — she rejoined the Cardews downstairs.

Soon she was seated at their table enjoying her first real meal in 3004. She found it delightful, the mysteriously created omelette having a richness of flavour that her own time had never been able to produce. This, the hot drink that tasted like a cross between cocoa and coffee, and the warm friendliness of the two who were her guardians, made her begin to feel almost happy again.

'You're more than kind,' Lucy smiled. 'One day, if I can ever convince the powers-that-be that I'm quite harmless, I'll try and get some work and repay you for all you've done.'

'Forget it,' Buck grinned. 'Only too glad to help. As for repayment, we won't even hear of it. You can help Eva if you like, as Worker Ten would have done, and let it go at that.'

Lucy nodded and then went on with her meal. During the course of it she gathered that there were two children in the Cardew family — boy and girl — but by law they were not allowed to live in the home during the 'education period.' They were cared for by the State crèche and only allowed, until the age of sixteen, to see their parents twice a year. In this manner juvenile delinquency had long since been stamped out even though it caused profound heartache amongst many parents.

By the time she had got to bed, between sheets electrically aired from a source she could not discover, Lucy was quite convinced that she was dreaming. Surely all this couldn't really be happening? Even now she had not assimilated the astounding fact that she would never see 2009 again ... Had she been in the office of the Master at that moment, however, she would certainly have realized that her experience was not a dream.

The Master, in fact, was by no means pleased at being detained so late in his lofty sanctuary. The power failure had delayed him in the first instance, and now the repercussions of it were still holding him to his desk. Before him stood a guard — the same one who had questioned Clem, Buck and Lucy on the river bridge.

'I've had the engineers throw a skeleton passway over the fissure, Master,' he reported. 'It will take all the traffic single-file. The bridge dissolution seems to have ceased now so I have given the order for traffic to resume. Parts of the faulty bridge section have been removed and sent to the analytical laboratory for a report.'

'Very well,' the Master acknowledged, making a note. 'I want an immediate report when the cause of the defect is known. You informed the laboratory of that, I trust?'

'I did, Master, yes.'

'Anything else?'

'Yes, Master. A public transport plunged over the fissure, and then a private auto-bus — '

'I know. That was reported direct. It has been given over the public speaker, together with a list of the numbers and names of the passengers. That was done for the convenience of relatives. The transport will be salvaged from the river in daylight, together with the private car that followed it. The occupants of that car are at present unidentified, I take it?'

'Up to the moment, Master, yes. There is, however, a matter I feel I should report. It puzzles me — '

The guard broke off in surprise as his atom gun holster, hanging from a broad strap about his shoulder, suddenly dropped to the floor. He gazed down at it blankly and the Master waited, his lips compressed.

'I would suggest that in future you buckle your accoutrements more securely,' he said curtly.

The guard nodded somewhat dazedly and picked up his gun and holster from the floor. The odd thing was that the strap was securely buckled — but the leather itself had rotted visibly close to the holster.

'Obtain a fresh one,' the Master instructed, studying it. 'Here is a renewal card — ' He handed it over and sat back in his chair. 'You were remarking upon a matter which puzzles you. Please continue.'

The guard came back to life with something of an effort. 'Er, yes,' he assented. 'It concerns a young woman whom I encountered on the bridge in company with Mister Bradley and Mister Cardew, the two blasting engineers who are at work on the Protection Tower foundations. She had no index-card with her, her explanation being that she had accidentally dropped it. Mister Bradley confirmed her statement. However, she gave her index-number as Worker Ten, Domestic Grade. Since then I have learned from the public transport authority that Worker Ten was on the transport which fell in the river.'

The Master drew towards him the passenger list, which had been submitted from transport headquarters. He studied it, then with no expression in his face he pushed it aside again.

'Yes, Worker Ten was on that transport,' he confirmed. 'That is if she did take it. Certainly her number was registered, as was everybody else's. There may be a mistake.'

'We could be sure, Master, if we had Worker Ten's civic photograph transmitted immediately. I could tell in a moment if the girl I saw is the same person.'

'Very well.' The Master touched a button and spoke into the microphone that swung gently towards him. 'Civic Records?' he asked. 'Transmit immediately a photograph of Worker Ten, female, Domestic Grade.'

'Yes, Master.'

There followed an interval, during which the guard carefully examined his mysteriously ruined gunbelt; then a screen came to life on the Master's desk and in vivid coloring Worker Ten was depicted, both full-face and profile. She was dark, thin-cheeked, with one eyebrow noticeably higher than the other.

'No,' the guard said flatly. 'That is not the woman I saw.'

The Master switched off, frowning a little. 'I assume you ordered her to report with her index-card by tomorrow?'

'I did, Master. I assumed her story to be genuine, but now I am extremely doubtful.'

'And you say she was with Mister Bradley and Mister Cardew?'

'Yes, Master. I recognized them immediately: their work makes them pretty well-known at present. That was why I gave her the benefit of the doubt.'

'Quite so. It is unlikely that Mister Bradley would take her to his home since he is known to be living alone at present. Mister Cardew, on the other hand, has a wife. You might do worse than make enquiry at Mister Cardew's home and get further details. If you fail in that respect then put a guard on all routes out of town and use a secondary investigation corps to keep watch on the homes of both Mister Cardew and Mister Bradley. Just at the moment we cannot afford any laxity with unidentified people. International tension is too great.'

'Very well, Master. I'll make enquiry immediately.'

The guard bowed his way out and departed. He stayed in the building only long enough to obtain a new belt from the armaments section, then he was on his way in an official car. His arrival at the Cardew home and subsequent hammering on the door stirred Buck out of well-earned slumber.

'What the hell — ' he growled, sitting up and listening. 'Who'd want me at this time of night?'

He was too fogged with sleep at that moment to think of anything but the blasting site being the cause of trouble. Then when he had stumbled to the window and saw a law officer looking up from the brightly-lighted street he remembered Lucy.

'Eva, quick!' he gasped hoarsely, and she stirred lazily in her bed. 'The police I think. Get Ancient to a safe place.'

'But — but where?' Eva groped stupidly for her robe.

'I dunno. Think of something. I'll keep this quizzer occupied meanwhile.'

Buck flung open the window and leaned out. 'Well, what is it?' he demanded — and Eva fled from the bedroom, reaching Lucy's room in a matter of seconds.

'Wass wrong?' Lucy yawned, awakened from a dream of 2008, in which she and Reggie had been enjoying a picnic. 'Who is it?'

'Eva! Get out of bed and follow me — and keep quiet!'

Strangeness in her surroundings caused her several moments' delay in focusing things. When at last she did get a grip on realities she realized she was being pushed relentlessly, along with the discarded clothes Eva had taken from her bedside, into the washing machine in the kitchen. The lights were not on and the whole thing was a confused struggle in semi-gloom.

'Police are here,' Eva panted, just visible in reflected street light from outside. 'This is the only place I can put you. Cover yourself with the clothes, and don't breathe, sneeze or move!'

The lid closed and Lucy crouched, cold metal fittings prodding into her in most uncomfortable places. She waited, her heart thudding.

'This is an absolute waste of time, officer,' came Buck's grumbling voice, as he led the way into the living room and switched on the lights. 'Digging me out at this hour with your crazy notions!'

Eva fled up the back stairs from the kitchen and regained Lucy's room. Hastily she remade the bed, removed the borrowed pair of shoes she had previously overlooked, and then hurried back with them to her own room.

'I'm acting under orders, Mister Cardew,' the guard said, his keen eyes darting about the room. 'You know as well as I do that we cannot afford to take chances these days, particularly with potential spies.'

'Spies!' Buck exclaimed. 'What in blazes do you mean? I assure you — '

'Look here, Mister Cardew, my time's valuable, and I know you must be wanting to get back to bed. Better let me search the place, then I can report back to headquarters.'

'Where's your authority?' Buck snapped — but in face of the official card the guard displayed he had no power to say anything further. Grim-faced and inwardly apprehensive he prowled directly behind the officer as he made a routine search of the downstairs rooms, until presently he reached the kitchen.

'Look, man, do you think I'd be idiot enough to try and house a spy?' Buck demanded.

'You might. Anybody might.' The guard's eyes pinned him. 'Sorry. No personal offence intended but anybody and everybody's suspect these days. The fact remains that the woman you were with on the bridge tonight, with Mister

Bradley was not Worker Ten.'

The guard peered inside the food-manufacturing machine and then eyed the washer thoughtfully. The small transparent inspection panel at the front showed only the borrowed clothes Lucy had hastily shoved in front of her. He strolled towards it and put his hand to the lid, then his attention was arrested by something in a wicker-basket in the corner. Moving over to it he lifted out a brown silk dress and other odds and ends of feminine finery, including an old-fashioned pair of shoes.

'What are these?' he asked curtly, as Buck stared at them.

'Eh? My wife's of course. Get your hands off them!'

'I want the truth, Mister Cardew. These garments cannot possibly be your wife's. I'm married myself and I know that no woman in her right senses wears this kind of thing now. Hundreds of years ago maybe, but not today. What's the answer?'

'We — er — ' Buck rubbed his neck. 'We've been putting over an amateur television play recently and an old-fashioned character was in it. That was the clothing my wife used.'

'I'd like the name of the play, the public access station from which it was televised, and a copy of the permit to present it.'

Buck became silent. His none too swift brain had run out of excuses.

'All very unconvincing, Mister Cardew,' the guard snapped. 'I have no proof, of course, that these extraordinarily old-fashioned clothes belong to the woman I'm looking for, but I will say that it's a reasonable assumption! Now, are you prepared to give me the facts and save yourself a great deal of trouble later?'

'There are no facts to give,' Buck retorted. 'And the sooner you get out of my house the better I'll like it.'

'I'll leave when my investigation is complete. Let us go upstairs.'

Bundling up the clothes the guard pushed them into a plastic bag, which Buck sullenly handed to him from a kitchen drawer, then the search continued upstairs. Eva, feigning sleep, felt her heart hammer as the guard switched on the light and went silently but thoroughly around the bedroom — then he came out again and looked at the adjoining door.

'What's in there?' he asked briefly.

'Vis — visitor's room.' Buck clenched his fists. He had no idea whether Lucy was in there or not.

'Open it.'

Buck obeyed and the lights came up. He sighed within himself at beholding everything orderly, the bed coverlet drawn up and giving a 'not-slept-in' appearance. The guard looked under the bed, then straightened and went to the wardrobe and slid back the door. The rails were empty.

'Very well,' he said, turning. 'I'll take a look at the other appointments in the house and then go — and I think you are a very foolish man, Mister Cardew. You will have to do a lot of thinking to explain away this!' and he held up the plastic bag significantly.

Buck did not answer. A glint of fury in his eyes he kept beside the guard until he had finally satisfied himself — so far as he could tell — that the girl he sought was nowhere in the house. Only then did he depart, and even then Buck waited until the noise of the official car died away in the distance.

'Blast!' he muttered to himself, and then at a sudden clangor from the kitchen he hurried in to find Lucy just disentangling herself from the washing-machine.

'Nice cold thing to hide in,' she panted as he helped her free.

'You — you were in there?' Buck gasped. 'Sweet cosmos, thank heaven he saw your old clothes, just as he was about to look in this washer.'

'My clothes?' Lucy's face tautened visibly.

'He took them, I'm afraid — and trouble will be bound to follow. We'd better go up and tell Eva just how we're fixed. Come along.'

They hurried upstairs together, in time to discover Eva just emerging from the bedroom.

'How's things?' she asked anxiously. 'I managed to get Lucy's room straight in time, but — '

'We're in trouble,' Buck broke in. 'Serious trouble — and I don't know how long it'll be before the storm breaks. I'd ring Clem and ask his advice only the lines might be tapped. Better sit tight till morning if we can.'

Meantime Clem was just being aroused by the zealous guard, and much the same routine was followed as at Buck's house. Clem, a far more wary man than Buck, made no statements at all. He had nothing to fear since his bachelor home was entirely deserted except for himself.

'Can you explain clothes belonging to a period many hundreds of years old being found in Mister Cardew's kitchen?' the guard asked, as he was about to leave. He jerked at the bag he was carrying.

'How can I?' Clem asked quietly. 'Buck Cardew may be my business partner but I don't know what he does with his private life. You're wasting your time asking, officer.'

'I never waste my time, Mister Bradley: I'm not allowed to. I am simply giving you the opportunity to explain away a woman with no index-card with whom you and Mister Cardew are definitely connected.'

'If I have anything to explain it will not be to you.'

The guard hesitated, then with a shrug he went on his way. He finished up at the Headquarters Building where he made out his report. There was nothing more he could do now until he could see the Master, and that would not be until morning.

When morning came he presented himself in the great and isolated sanctuary far above the town, clutching his plastic bag. The Master, looking not in the least refreshed after a night's sleep, eyed him questioningly, 'Reporting investigation into mystery of Worker Ten, Master, as instructed,' the guard explained.

'Ah, yes. I would remark that guards are supposed to be spruce and freshly-shaved. You are a disgrace to your uniform!'

'I apologize, Master. This matter is so very urgent. I have not located the woman we're seeking, but I did find these articles of feminine apparel in Mister Cardew's home, pushed into a clothes-basket. The significant thing is that the clothes belong

90

to a period of many centuries ago, so I am at a loss to understand it. See for yourself, Master.'

Eagerly the guard opened the hermetically self-sealed bag top and tipped it upside down over a clear space on the desk. Shaking vigorously he watched for the clothes to tumble out . . . instead there was a sigh of escaping air — which had caused the bag to retain its shape overnight — and what appeared to be a cloud of dust, which dissipated as the air escaped from the bag. Otherwise the bag was completely empty.

'Well?' The Master raised his eyebrows.

'I — I just don't understand it, Master! This bag has never left me all night. There was a dress and — and other things, a pair of ancient shoes too, and a belt . . . '

Silence. Then the Master sat back in his chair. 'I would suggest you shave,' he said, 'and then, when you have thoroughly cleared your mind, come back and explain. This kind of work will not do you any good, Officer Sixty-Seven. That is all.'

'But, Master, I tell you — '

'That — is all!'

4

Age!

In the east of the great city the experts in the analytical laboratory were at work. Under intensely powerful lights and surrounded with instruments, they had sections of the steel which had proved faulty in the great Mid-City Bridge, and the more they examined the metal the more puzzled they became.

Barnes, leading technician of the group, finally summed the whole analysis up in one word.

'Age!' he said, and gave a bewildered glance at the men around him.

'That's what it looks like, but it's incredible,' declared Forsythe. 'This sort of steel, the same as we use on our cannon-ball express train tracks, is tested to the limit and it certainly wasn't cast more than a hundred-and-fifty years ago. Then there's been regular overhauling — '

'The fact remains,' Barnes interrupted irritably, 'that age is the cause of this trouble. The metal itself has corroded away. It's like a rotten biscuit inside. Honeycombed and crawling with advanced ferrous oxide decay. That means age no matter how you look at it.'

'And the same thing can be said of that flywheel which burst apart in the power house,' remarked Dawlish, head of the metallurgy branch. 'Take a look at this sample: it's from the flywheel.'

The puzzled but interested men peered at it as it lay in the scientist's hand, and there was no gainsaying the fact that it had the same 'honeycomb' texture as the steel from the bridge. It looked exactly like wood that has been eaten through by white ants.

'Well,' Barnes said at length, 'we've found the reason even if we can't explain how it occurred. Only answer I can think of is sabotage. Maybe the Eastern agents are using some kind of electronic device, which rots the composition of metals. We'd better report it to the Master and let him take the responsibility. After all, we're not magicians . . . '

So the Master was informed and brooded, definitely perplexed, over the problem. He had good reason for being worried, for the case of the flywheel and the Mid-City Bridge was not the only one before him for consideration. In more than a dozen places steel had behaved contrary to law. In fact, several buildings had been endangered by the mysterious collapse of some of their supporting girders. The railroads too had experienced two disasters caused by the rotting of certain sections of the rails.

Finally the Master called a conference, in mid-morning, and attending it were all the men charged with keeping law and order throughout the city and the western hemisphere generally. They waited for the tired man at the desk to speak. After surveying his reports, he spoke quietly. 'Gentlemen, we have in our midst a group of ruthless saboteurs who are doing their best to wreck our utilities and our morale. What is more, if they keep on successfully practicing their diabolical art, they will succeed in their object. The people, not unnaturally, are raising a storm of protest over these mysterious and dangerous happenings. Somehow we have got to get to the root of this insidious attack and smash the perpetrators!'

'Do you suspect Eastern agent saboteurs, Master?' asked the Chief of A-Law Division.

'I do.' The Master inclined his head. 'Since this meeting is strictly secret I can air my views freely without the fear of international repercussions. I suspect the East most strongly, yes, because war with that hemisphere is unpleasantly imminent. The Eastern Government, so our ambassador tells me, is becoming more vociferous every day in its demands for certain illegal claims to be met. However, it would obviously suit them perfectly if we could be thrown into a state of confusion by the subtle wrecking of our lines of communication and the morale of our people. Somewhere agents are at work with scientific equipment that eats away steel. I have reason to suspect one particular woman, but she alone cannot be responsible for such widely spaced incidents. She must be one of hundreds. Use every means in your power to detect these wreckers. We must get this thing stopped!'

With this admonition ringing in their ears, the men departed to their different sectors to formulate plans. All of them were worried, and the Master most of all since his was the major responsibility.

There was also a very worried man to the north of the city, and his troubles were not even remotely connected with steel.

Caleb Walsh was a master-agriculturist. Under his care, Government-controlled, were some thousands of acres of crops and foodstuffs in the raw state. He was also responsible for extra hard beechwood trees, which formed the basis of many things even in this age of metals and plastics. And, at the moment, it was an area of two-hundred beechwood saplings, nurtured by artificial sunlight and fertilizers, which was worrying him. The previous day he had been convinced they were thriving almost too well to be normal. Now, this morning, as he went on his rounds, he was sure of it. At the sound of smashing glass behind him he wheeled round and then fell back, astounded.

Four of the tender saplings had abruptly grown to titanic proportions and smashed their way through the lofty glass roof. It was impossible! Yet it was there.

Walsh went forward slowly, swallowing hard, staring up at the giants rearing through the broken glass. Their side branches, too, had thrust forth incredibly and smashed down all the young trees in the neighboring area.

So much Walsh took in and then he raced for a visiphone and lifted it with a hand that shook. He made a report in a cracked voice to the Controller for Agriculture. The Controller listened sympathetically because it was not the only report he had received that morning. From all parts of the country within a hundred-mile radius of the city, it appeared, news kept coming in of beech trees becoming mysteriously hypertrophied.

There was, for instance, a beech tree at an old-world farm some distance out of town. With his own eyes the astounded owner had seen it rear from a tiny sapling against the moonlight to a mammoth giant overshadowing his house. Being a somewhat old-fashioned man he wondered if, after all, there had been some truth in Jack and the Beanstalk . . .

Once again, the Master found himself surrounded by his new set of problems and his face became grayer than ever as he tried to cope with them. That saboteurs could tamper with steel was a logical possibility, but that they could make beech trees grow to fantastic size within a period of minutes was neither logical nor sensible. No agent, surely, would waste time on such a fantastic and pointless diversion?

Inevitably, the facts about the beech trees leaked out, as did the news of collapsing buildings and dissolved railroad tracks. Clem Bradley heard the details when he arrived at the Cardew home in mid-morning. He, Buck, Lucy and Eva all listened to the information being given over the public broadcast.

'At the wish of the Master,' the announcer said, 'the public is asked to keep calm in face of mysterious happenings around us. The collapse of the Mid-City Bridge has been followed by other incidents, equally peculiar, in which the steel girders of buildings and the permanent way of a main railroad track have been involved. Analysts are now at work on the problem and a speedy solution is anticipated. Another unusual item, which can hardly have any relation to the odd behavior of steel, is contained in a report from the Agricultural Controller in which he states that certain beechwood trees under his jurisdiction have suddenly assumed gigantic proportions. Various possibilities can be conjectured for these bizarre happenings, and — '

'We've more things to do than listen to this,' Buck said briefly, speaking above the announcer's voice. 'Did you manage to get here safely, Clem? You weren't watched, or anything?'

'Of that I can't be sure. I'm hoping for

99

the best. Best thing we can do is whip along to the underground site and, once there, we can defy all-comers. I gather you had a visit from our zealous friend the guard during the night?'

Eva grimaced. 'We certainly did. Fun and games were had by all.'

'He tackled me too, and got nothing out of it. But he did ask about some old-fashioned clothes, which I suppose were yours, Lucy?'

The girl nodded and Buck gave an anxious glance. 'That's the part I don't like,' he said. 'Once the Master takes a look at those clothes the inquiry will intensify and then we'll be — '

'The answer to that is to get out while we can,' Clem interrupted. 'You'll have to do without your domestic help, Eva, I'm afraid.'

'Of course,' she assented, unable to disguise her relief at getting Lucy off the premises.

'You'd better get ready, Ancient,' Buck added. 'Put on your overalls.'

Lucy nodded and then hurried away. Buck gave a thoughtful glance towards the public speaker. The announcements had now ceased.

'What do you make of things, Clem?' he asked, puzzled. 'The queer antics of beech trees, for instance? Surely Eastern sabotage can't be responsible for that?'

'Hardly,' Clem answered absently, and with an abstracted look in his eyes he watched Eva hand over to Buck one of her own belts.

'This do until I can get you a fresh one later today?' she asked.

'Perfect,' Buck grinned. 'Even if I do feel a bit of a she-boy wearing it.'

He buckled it into place about the top of his trousers and Clem watched the proceeding with interest.

'What's wrong with your own?' he questioned.

'Bust! Rotted away down the back for no reason. It went last night.'

'Oh?' Clem's expression changed a little, but whatever he was intending to say did not materialize for at that moment Lucy came hurrying back, wrapped in her overalls.

'Right!' Buck said. 'Let's be on our way

before it dawns on somebody to try and stop us. What about a car, Clem? Got one fixed?'

'Yes, it's outside. My compensation claim was allowed right away and I've a far better car now than I had before. Come on.'

They took their leave of Eva and hurried outside, glancing to right and left along the traffic-way. There was no sign of official cars, and even less of watchers. They could not know, of course, that officialdom was concerning itself with the departure routes from town, along which people must pass to leave the city. Because of this, pinpointing of a suspect was unnecessary.

So, a little more confident, Clem settled at the car switchboard and started up the power. For the first few miles all went well, then he gave a grim glance at Buck as, ahead, there loomed an armed cordon guarding a barrier. Each autobus or pedestrian going through was being stopped, obviously for presentation of index-cards.

'Hell, we've driven right into it,' Buck

muttered. 'And no way back either,' he added, glancing at the stream of traffic banked up to the rear.

'Have to bluff our way through as best we can, that's all,' Clem said. 'No more than I expected would happen. We'll get by — somehow.'

As they moved closer to the barrier all hope collapsed.

The guard in charge was the same one they had encountered at their homes during the night, and he was still smarting under the Master's sarcasm at the unexpected disappearance of a number of feminine garments.

'Oh, you again!' he exclaimed, as he beheld the three in the new autobus. 'And you — !' He looked at Lucy.

'Last night you said you were Worker Ten and, so far, you haven't reported to headquarters to verify that fact. We happen to know that Worker Ten is dead, so what is your explanation?'

'Mistaken identity,' Clem said frankly.

'You mean spying! This woman's responsible among others for corroding steel, crazy beech trees, rotting leather, and a host of — '

'Rotting leather?' Clem repeated, surprised. 'Who told you about his pants' belt?' and he looked at Buck.

'Pants' belt?' The guard stared. 'I'm talking about my gun-holster strap!' he roared. 'Even that isn't safe from these damned spies! It broke without reason when I was standing right in front of the Master! And this morning, not half an hour ago, my boots broke in two! Better start explaining things, you,' he went on, glaring at Lucy. 'There's some low-down trickery going on and if anybody can say what it's all about it's you!'

'But — but I can't!' Lucy stammered, glancing back nervously as traffic to the rear kept a continuous chorus of siren blowing at the long delay.

'And those clothes I took!' the guard fumed. 'They were yours, weren't they? Weren't they?'

'Yes — yes,' Lucy agreed nervously.

'I thought so! Then you tell me why they disappeared from their bag without anybody being near them! No clothes can do that ordinarily! I hardly knew it had happened, because being silk they were light, but they went, and I want to know why!'

'I can't explain it,' Lucy protested. 'Honest I can't.'

The guard narrowed his eyes and whipped out his atom-gun. 'Out of that car!' he ordered. 'All of you. It's time the Master had a talk with — '

Then Buck's mighty fist lashed up suddenly and slammed straight into the guard's face. He howled with pain and went flying backwards, collapsing some six feet away. Without a second's pause Clem flung in the car switches and sent the vehicle flashing forward.

It whipped through the scattering line of officers clutching at their atom-guns. Within seconds they were left behind. Clinging to the steering-gear Clem stared ahead of him fixedly, dodging around and behind the traffic in front of him. Then at last he managed to merge the vehicle into the swirling tide of autobuses and transports flowing out of the city's heart.

'I hope you realize what sort of a mess we can get into now,' he panted, glancing at Buck. 'We'll be tracked down for hitting an officer.'

'Give them a run for their money, anyway,' Buck retorted. 'Better all three of us get arrested than just Ancient.'

Clem became silent, mainly because he inwardly agreed with his tough, impulsive friend. Lucy herself did not say anything. She sat with tight lips between the two men, realizing more than ever the complicated, dangerous tangle she had plunged into since arriving in 3004.

'Okay, here we go,' Clem said at length, and twisted the car off into a side-alley, thereby joining up with the normal route beyond the sundered bridge. Continuing at the same terrific speed it was not long before he gained the immense underground ramp, which led to the site of the Protection Tower foundations.

Once below, speeding through the long tunnels, all three began to breathe more freely.

'All right so far,' Clem said grimly, clambering out at last. 'Get the boys to work, Buck. Just at this moment I've got some figuring to do. If it works out right it may save us from the lethal chamber.'

'Eh?' Buck asked blankly. 'Figuring? What sort of figuring?'

'Well, let's say itemizing. I'll need you to help me, Lucy. Carry on, Buck. I'm staying right here. I want to get any news reports that may come through.'

Though he was clearly bewildered Buck did as he was told. Clem watched him heading away towards the site of operations, then he took the girl's arm and led her into the portable little building which served as a headquarters. He motioned her to a chair and she sat down.

'Lucy,' he said quietly, regarding her, 'I'm forming a most extraordinary theory about you — and it is the fact that it may be right that frightens me.'

'Frightens you?' Lucy's eyes were wide. 'W-why?'

'I have the feeling,' Clem continued, 'that some of the amazing things which keep happening may be directly attributable to you. The steel bridge, the beech trees, even Buck's pants' belt and the guard's holster belt.'

'Attributable to me? That's impossible! Clem, what in the world are you talking about?'

'A scientific possibility,' he replied, musing. 'As you know I am a scientist, though I don't pretend to be an extremely good one. Like all scientists, though, I get ideas and like to work on them. Now, let me do a bit of notating.'

From the desk he picked up a notebook and began to write down various items. Lucy watched as the words appeared under his swift handwriting-:

Steel Bridge.
Steel Flywheel.
Steel Building Supports.
Beech Trees.
Leather Belts and Boots (Guard's)
Silk Clothes.

'What's all that for?' Lucy enquired.

'I'm just listing the things that have been affected strangely. Tell me, those clothes of which you rid yourself, were they all silk? Every one of them?'

'Yes. Even the stockings.'

'I see. That seems to suggest that — '

Clem thought for a moment and then changed the subject. 'How many clothes are you wearing now that you wore in your own time?'

'None. Mrs. Cardew supplied everything I've got, including undergarments . . . '

Clem made a whistling noise with his teeth. 'Things are getting awfully complicated,' he said. 'If I can only find the right scientific relationship to explain all this I'll be able to prove to the hilt that you really are a girl from the past. Then the Master will not only believe you, he'll honor you. I only hope you don't cause too much trouble in the meantime.'

'Trouble?' Lucy repeated. 'But, Clem, the very last thing I want to do is cause trouble to anybody.'

'Not you personally, I don't mean — but the various things connected with you — '

Clem broke off and glanced towards the civic loudspeaker as it came to life. First came a dreary routine statement of city matters, and then the announcer continued: 'A series of incidents, which may be considered either ludicrous or alarming, depending upon how one looks at it, are reported from various centers this morning. Many men and women, for instance, have found themselves suddenly without any footwear, their boots and shoes have either crumbled to powder in certain sections or, in more extreme cases have vanished entirely without explanation! Similar things have happened to men's and women's belts and to handbags, briefcases, and even leather trunks . . . '

Clem crouched in silence at the desk, listening. Lucy was staring at the loudspeaker as though she were paralyzed.

'A further case is reported of General Brandon Urston who examining our defenses in case of Eastern invasion, found himself with his ray-gun charges, and the charges themselves, lying on the ground. Every supporting belt had gone. From Sector Fifty there is news of a cattle disease. It appears that pigs, cows, bulls, oxen, and various other species of animals are dying. The disease seems to be a form of rapid senility, followed in most cases by actual disintegration, which so far has the veterinary experts and scientists baffled ... Stand by please for Regulation Announcements.'

Clem looked at the girl steadily and her eyes met his in wonder. 'Lucy, my dear, you are a very dangerous person,' he said at last. 'And the unique thing about it is that you don't realize it! Let me think! I must get this lot into bright focus before I dare approach the Master ... '

*   *   *

On the other side of the world, Leslie Hurst, ambassador for the West, had been summoned to an audience with Lan Ilof, the President of the Eastern Council.

President Ilof was not alone in his office. In the heavy chairs close beside his big desk sat the grim-faced General Zoam and General Niol. They sat eyeing Ambassador Hurst as he came in.

'Do sit down, Ambassador.' The President moved a hand and smiled cordially. 'How are you?'

'I can hardly imagine, Mister President,

that you sent for me to enquire after my welfare,' Hurst answered. 'May I ask that you state your business?'

'It hardly needs a statement, Mister Hurst. More, shall we say, a reiteration? I wish to point out that you have been most dilatory in regard to answering our claim for a half share in the planet Mars.'

'Kindly accept my apologies,' Hurst replied. 'It is not that I have been dilatory: I have simply had no statement to make. The Master of our Western peoples has made it perfectly clear, I think, that he will have no part in interplanetary blackmail.'

'How dare you insult the President in that fashion?' demanded General Niol, springing up. 'The least the Master of the West can do is make a courteous reply to a demand. He has not even done that!'

'He will hardly consider it necessary when I have conveyed his answer,' Hurst retorted. 'Since, gentlemen, we seem to have at last arrived at the point where we are putting our cards on the table, let me state now, unequivocally that the Master of the West will not entertain your claim regarding Mars. Not only is such a claim utterly without foundation, but you do not even produce convincing evidence to support it. Certainly one cannot regard photographs and other supposed records as proof.'

'You have been given an ultimatum,' General Zoam snapped. 'It should be either accepted or rejected in the normal diplomatic fashion.'

'Ultimatum?' Hurst looked surprised. 'When?'

'Now! Surely you of the West are not so dense that you cannot recognize an ultimatum when you get it? In more direct terms, Ambassador Hurst, we either have the Master of the West's recognition of our legal rights concerning Mars, or else we shall act by force and take what belongs to us. Is that sufficiently plain?'

'You mean war,' Hurst said quietly.

'Exactly,' General Niol retorted. 'We suspected from the very start that it would come to it finally — and now it almost has. It is up to the Master of the West whether or not the fuse is lighted.'

113

Hurst's eyes shifted to President Ilof. He was sitting in silence, musing. He looked up as Hurst asked a direct question.

'Are you in agreement with war to solve the problem, Mister President? Or do you believe, as I do, that such a step could only end in appalling carnage with nothing achieved by either side?'

'We have nothing to fear,' the President answered, and it was more than obvious he was doing his utmost to avoid offending the Generals on either side of him. 'Our armaments are powerful and our cause just. We have no intention of being ruled any longer by the dictates of the West.'

'Even though we are all essentially the same people? Centuries of intermarriage has eliminated all the racial tensions of the old millennium and brought peace to the Earth. Do you really want to return to that barbaric period in our history? I can't believe it.'

The President was silent, apparently trying to think of a suitable answer. Then General Niol answered for him. 'The sooner you understand, Mister Hurst, that there is no sentiment in the satisfying of legal and rightful claims, the better! We are determined to take half of Mars, either by agreement or by force. Kindly transmit that information to the Master of the West.'

'I would be wasting my time. He has already given his answer — and it is that he will not yield a fraction of Martian territory to you or anybody else.'

The two men of war looked at the President, and he made no attempt to disguise the troubled look upon his face.

'I am sorry, Mister Hurst, deeply sorry, that things have come to this,' he said seriously. 'Up to now our relationship has been most cordial, but, as you will appreciate, in matters of interplanetary or international politics, there can be no personal feeling. I personally am deeply sorry to have to ask you to close down your Embassy Office within twenty-four hours and return to your own hemisphere.'

'You mean break off relations?' Hurst asked. 'That is the overture to war, Mister President.'

'I am aware of it. You will be given time to arrive home safely. After that force of arms alone can decide the issue.'

Hurst rose, looked at the two grimly satisfied Generals, and then went on his way. The moment he arrived in his headquarters in another section of the Eastern capital city he contacted the Master on the private waveband that was immune from 'tapping'.

'Master?' he enquired, as the Master's voice answered. 'I am afraid the worst has happened. War is more or less inevitable with the East, and in a very short time. Maybe a week — possibly less. I have been ordered to close down my Embassy office and return to the West in twenty-four hours. Before complete calamity befalls have you any fresh instructions? Any concessions you wish to make?'

'I never make concessions, Ambassador Hurst, and I never reverse my decisions. You will return to here as ordered, and I will handle the situation. Immediate steps will be taken for us to stand by our defenses.'

'Very well, sir,' Hurst answered, sighing

to himself, and with that he switched off.
Then he turned his attention to collecting
his documents and informing his staff of
what was intended.

5

Vanishing cargo

Commander Brian Neil intently watched the directional compass needle and then frowned to himself. Finally he checked it with a subsidiary compass and frowned all the more. There was no doubt about it: the two compasses were completely at variance. One — the normal one — pointed vaguely to the east, whereas it should have pointed directly to the north magnetic pole and acted thereby as a course-finder. The subsidiary one did point in that direction and was behaving according to plan.

'What do you make of this, Mister Swanton?' Neil asked his chief navigator finally.

Swanton came over from surveying the oceanic charts and gave the compass his expert scrutiny. 'Main compass broken down, sir,' he replied finally. 'Fortunately the subsidiary one seems to be working normally.'

'That compass,' Commander Neil said, 'is one of the best products Enzon and Balro have ever turned out, and worth a fortune. Better dismantle it and see what's wrong. If the subsidiary one goes wrong too we'll be in a mess.'

'Very good, sir.'

Navigator Swanton went to work with practiced hands, removing the compass from its heavy casement. Meanwhile Commander Neil took over the task of steering the vessel across the wastes of the Atlantic ocean.

As he gazed out on the deeps, or consulted the multitude of instruments by which he guided the vessel through treacherous cross-currents, Neil smiled to himself, his mind jumping for a moment to the storeroom where there reposed crates of electrical machinery and silk-worms. He wondered how the Controller of Exports had ever conceived the idea that such a cargo might be stolen or tampered with. It was absurd! Out here in the middle of the ocean no pirate could attack without being seen long before he arrived; and the crew of the vessel was a good one, every man as honest as the sunlight.

'Here's the trouble, sir,' Swanton said finally, and Neil looked at the bench before him upon which the navigator had laid the 'insides' of the compass. The main bearing had completely corroded — it was made of steel — and the sockets into which it was delicately fitted were covered with a fine reddish dust.

'The corrosion of this steel spindle is a real mystery,' Swanton commented. 'This sort of steel has a guaranteed life of two-hundred-and-fifty years. The date stamp on this compass is one year ago when the switchboard was refitted. I fancy, sir, that Enzon and Balro are going to develop a lot of gray hairs over this!'

Neil mused for a moment as he looked out onto the heaving ocean.

'Come to think of it,' he said at length, 'I've heard rumors whilst we were ashore concerning strange behavior by steel — but I never thought it would catch up on our compass like this!'

'Very extraordinary, sir,' the navigator agreed, and set the ruined compass on one side. 'I hope our other one doesn't go the same way!'

That seemed to end the subject, mainly because it was too bewildering a problem to pursue. Neil re-checked the course by the subsidiary compass, and then glanced at the chronometer.

'Take over, Mister Swanton,' he ordered. 'My rest period is due.'

'Very good, sir.'

On his way from the bridge to his cabin, Neil paused for a moment by the steel door of the storage-hold and considered. He recalled the puzzling admonition he had received from the Export manager, respecting his cargo.

He half moved on and then hesitated. Might as well satisfy himself. So, using his memory for the combination lock he unfastened it and swung open the storage-hold door. The hundred cases of electrical machinery and sixty of silk-worms were still there. Those containing the machinery had small inspection holes in the sides — and those containing the silkworms had filters so they could breathe.

Neil glanced through the nearest inspection plate on the crates containing machinery. Then he looked again with more urgency. Startled, he peered inside the next crate, and then the next. Thoroughly alarmed he jumped across to where the crates of silkworms stood and the answer was even more startling. There was only one thing to do to satisfy himself, and he did it. He wrenched the lids from the nearest crates and then let them fall with a clatter, his senses completely stunned by the vision of a pile of completely broken and jumbled components smothered in rust in the machinery crates. As for the silkworms, these crates were completely empty. Not a vestige, not a trace!

Aware of the recent international tensions, his mind revolved round spies, saboteurs, even plain unvarnished magic; then commonsense stepped in and took charge. Returning to the bridge control-room he had the freighter stopped so that the engineers could leave their posts.

Then, with the few others essential to the crew, he had them assemble in the bridge.

'I am not going to beat about the bush, men,' he said, coming straight to the point. 'I am going to give the culprit amongst you the chance to confess and save a lot of trouble. To state the matter briefly, a consignment of machinery and silkworms, our cargo for Brazil, has been broken and corroded into useless junk in the case of the machinery, whilst the silkworms have vanished completely. The crates have apparently not been opened, but the contents have nevertheless been tampered with or removed completely. As far as I know I am the only person with the combination of the storage-room door, but obviously someone else has gained knowledge of that combination. Now, which of you is going to speak?'

Nobody did. They looked completely astonished. It was noteworthy that not a single man had an angry look. Commander Neil was too much respected for any member of his crew to show open resentment.

'If I might say something, sir?' asked

Andrews, the first mate.

'Well?' Neil barked.

'What man would want silkworms, and what man could destroy machinery without being heard and apprehended? The very idea of it is absurd, sir — meaning no disrespect.'

'There are ways of doing so, Andrews, if the occasion warrants it,' Neil snapped.

'I don't see how such a thing could happen, sir,' Swanton remarked. 'Both consignments were safely in the vessel when we disembarked: you told me you'd checked on them. That could only mean the depredations and theft took place whilst we were in mid-ocean. And that is equally impossible. No vessel has been anywhere near us to take off stolen cargo, and for one of us to remove the silkworms from their crates and throw them overboard simply doesn't make sense.'

'True,' Neil admitted, thinking, for fortunately he was not an obstinate man. He was always ready to listen to anything reasonable when a problem baffled him.

'Do I understand, sir, that the crates themselves have not been disturbed?'

Swanton continued.

'Correct. From the look of them the crates themselves have not been disturbed. Theoretically, of course, it is possible to remove an object from inside another by fourth dimensional processes, and in this scientific era I am willing to believe that it could be done. An experienced spy might have knowledge enough to do it.'

'I don't agree, sir,' Swanton said. 'A spy would never trouble to be so complicated. If he knew the combination of the storage-hold door he would most certainly get rid of the cargo by dispatching it somewhere in the crates. You have entirely the wrong angle, or so I think.'

Neil frowned and moved to the starboard outlook, gazing out for a time over the rolling ocean. Finally he turned.

'Mister Swanton . . .'

'Sir?'

'Take Mister Carlton with you and search the ship. The cargo may be concealed somewhere. The rest of you men stay here until the search is completed.'

The order was promptly obeyed, and for close on twenty minutes Swanton and Carlton, the chief engineer, were absent. When they came back they merely shrugged their shoulders.

'Not a trace, sir,' Swanton said. 'And if I may say so the concealment of large amounts of live silkworms is hardly an easy task.'

'I'll be made to look about the biggest fool in the service, when I radio my report back to my employers,' Neil declared bitterly. 'To continue to Brazil now is useless since we haven't a cargo to deliver! And what sort of a story am I to tell them back home? That the cargo was trashed or vanished from under my very nose without any explanation?'

'There must be an explanation,' Swanton muttered, his brows knitted.

'Then I'd be glad if you'd find it for I certainly can't. All right, men, back to your posts. We're returning to Bristol immediately, and I warn you there will be a most rigid enquiry. That consignment was of extreme value. Take over, Mister Swanton. I am still entitled to sleep even if the damned cargo does disappear!'

And, fuming with anger, Neil followed the baffled crew from the bridge. Before heading for his cabin he detoured to the radio room and made his report.

And, like all similar odd reports it was subsequently transmitted to the office of the Master, and became one more story in an accumulating pile of them that just cried out for a sensible answer.

The Master, in fact, sifted these stories and reports for the best part of the following morning. Amongst them was the report from Commander Neil explaining that his cargo of machinery had been destroyed, and that of silkworms had vanished without trace. He was willing to resign the service in disgrace because he just could not explain the mystery.

'The problems are not isolated,' the Master muttered to himself. 'Therein lies the mystery of it all. Steel supports have collapsed in countless places, and machinery and vital instruments containing steel have rotted and fallen apart. Then there are numerous instances of silk garments that have rotted and developed holes or disappeared altogether. On top of that is corroding leather, dying animals that subsequently disappear leaving only bones, warps in beechwood and devastating increase in the size of some beech trees . . . ' He drew a hand over his face wearily as he looked at the reports. 'All this cannot be the work of spies, surely?'

He sat for a long time, thinking, turning the mystery over in his mind, but scientist though he was even he could not work without a known premise or fact from which to start. So, gradually, his thoughts drifted back to one recollection — that of the guard who had found clothes belonging to a period many centuries earlier, and then had discovered their entire disappearance. And they had belonged to a woman who had not been identified, and Clem Bradley and Buck Cardew possibly knew a good deal about her.

His face grim the Master flicked a switch and spoke. 'Find Boring Engineers Bradley and Cardew at the Protection Tower site and order them to come here without delay. If they refuse, use force.

And with them bring, if possible, a woman worker whom they are shielding.'

'Yes, Master.'

The information was promptly passed to the appropriate quarter, and it happened to be Guard Sixty-Seven who was on duty when the order came through. So far he had not reported that he had been hit in the face and that Cardew, Clem and the mystery girl had got away from him: he didn't wish to take the risk on top of having already failed to produce the clothes after the song he had made about them. But this new order looked like his supreme chance to clean matters up. His eyes narrowed, he gave orders to his men and promptly went into action.

In consequence he and his fellow guards appeared suddenly in the underground workings of the Protection Tower, towards the close of the afternoon. Clem and Buck were not expecting such a thing to happen and were overpowered before they could make an attempt to save themselves.

'What the devil's the idea?' Clem

demanded hotly. 'Or don't you know I'm in charge down here?'

'Not as far as the law is concerned,' the guard answered, with a sour glance. 'I've been waiting for a chance like this, Mister Bradley, to even up the score — and now I've got it! Where is that woman you brought with you?'

'What woman?' Buck asked innocently.

'You know perfectly well! The one who was with you in your autobus this morning.'

'Suppose you try and find out?' Clem suggested. 'She is quite innocent of any crime, no matter what the law thinks or does — and she'll stay safely hidden. Understand?'

'You're a fool,' Guard Sixty Seven said. 'She'll be found! Search the place,' he added to his men.

Clem gave Buck a significant glance. The girl, concealed in a high niche of the wilderness of working, was not likely to even be seen, let alone captured, and the boys on the job would see that she was kept safe and well provisioned since they were completely loyal to their two bosses.

'All right, let's be on our way,' the guard snapped at last. 'We can't hang about forever. Get a move on, you two! For the time being you can consider yourselves under arrest, by order of the Master.'

He led the way to the official autobus in the tunnel and in a few minutes it was whirling them through the city again. So, at length, Clem and Buck found themselves in the austere presence of the Master.

'You may go,' he told the guards; then his thin hand reached out and pressed a button so that the entire interview might be recorded for later playback and study.

'Sit down, gentlemen,' he invited, and both men looked surprised.

'I was given to understand by the guard, sir, that we are prisoners,' Clem remarked.

'Guard Sixty-Seven is hardly a man of discernment, Mister Bradley,' the Master answered dryly. 'You are not prisoners — yet. I simply wish to ask you a few questions, and you will be good enough not to be evasive with your answers.

There are limits to my patience with the number of problems I have on my mind.'

Clem sat down slowly and so did Buck, his big jaw jutting obstinately.

'Now . . . ' The Master relaxed in his chair, 'what is your explanation, gentlemen, for shielding a woman from the authorities because she has no index-card? What is this mystery woman's connection with mysterious acts of sabotage which began from the time she was first noticed?'

Clem hesitated for a long moment, then he said deliberately, 'That woman, Master, is named Lucy Denby. She came from the year 2009.'

'I warned you, Mister Bradley, that my patience is wearing thin. To the point, please!'

'That is the truth, sir. And it is because she has come from 2009 that so many queer things keep happening.'

'I can understand that she is probably at the back of the many mysterious incidents besetting us, but I certainly do not believe that she comes from a time of a thousand years ago. Our best scientists have proven time travel — in a physical form at least — to be impossible.'

'I am aware of it, Master, but you would not deny that a person could, by scientific means, be physically suspended for a thousand years and awaken in perfect health, would you?'

'Well — no.' The Master frowned. 'You mean this woman slept for almost a thousand years?'

'She didn't exactly sleep. Because of entropy being fully created she leapt the time-gap without being aware that she had leapt it.'

The Master made a weary movement. 'Mister Bradley, I am a very tired man, and I am in no mood to ponder such outrageous theories at the moment. This much I will tell you — then you may realize the seriousness of your behavior. Our ambassador to the East informs me that Eastern invasion is imminent within a day or two. This hemisphere of ours is faced by an onslaught from the most efficient scientific armada in history, and it is horribly possible that we may be utterly defeated. The West is riddled with spies, of which this woman — who has evidently fooled you into thinking she is a denizen of a thousand years ago — is a particularly blundering example. Only since her appearance has steel developed such grave faults, a vital ingredient of our infrastructure and armaments. Beechwood, and beech trees, leather — those, too, have been queerly affected, obviously by atomic control. I remain convinced this woman can explain the mystery even if she did not actually participate in the sabotage. I would also ask her, could I find her, how she, or her contemporaries, destroyed a valuable cargo of machinery and silkworms from a freight vessel at sea. Silk is also being treated strangely, Mister Bradley, and of course it is a valuable armament ingredient, apart from its use for clothing — '

'That's it — silkworms!' Clem cried in excitement. 'That fits in! I do believe my theory is right!'

The Master frowned. 'What theory?'

'I've been working one out, sir, and I needed a few more factors to make it fit.

And now I think it does! But first may I ask if you will please at least listen to the story of this woman, and how I came to discover her in a sealed globe.'

'Proceed,' the Master invited, and half-closed his eyes in order to concentrate.

'As I see it,' Clem said, when he had outlined the earlier details of the finding of Lucy in the force-globe, 'that scientist, Bryce Fairfield, forgot something, and it was this: If you place anything organic or inorganic in a field of non-time you destroy the entropy. Everything in the bubble was stopped dead in its tracks. No entropy went on at all, but each article in the bubble gave off the energy that we recognize as entropy. Therefore the energy was still there, but imprisoned.'

'And so?' the Master asked.

'For a thousand years,' Clem continued, 'a girl in silk clothes lay on a steel table. She was cradled about the head and shoulders in a beechwood rack and fastened down by heavy leather straps. All these things I noticed when I first saw her through the globe.

135

You begin to understand, sir? For a thousand years the energy of everything about her was emanated, but it could not escape. Entropy was there but held stagnant. Hence, when the globe was finally shattered the energy of entropy-change went forth in an overpowering wave and sought out the original atomic formation from which it had sprung, just as a river takes the shortest route to the sea. It had to do so in order to catch up on the predestined entropy intended for those particular formations.

'So, Master, steel in the Mid-City Bridge went soft because of extreme age and the strain it was taking. It affected the steel of my brake pedal also. Why? Because the steel that formed the girl's table came from the same ores that were later used to make a bridge. Metals, like human beings, exist in groups from a parent set of ores — but the parts of the bridge made from a different set of ores were unaffected. Everything connected with the girl suddenly became a thousand years old! Beech trees shot up to a thousand years of growth because those particular trees were direct descendants of the tree from which the head cradle had been made.

'Leather disappeared because it was made from the skin of animals whose ancestors had provided the leather for the straps and the belt on the girl's frock. Live animal ancestors also suddenly became a thousand years old. It would operate through the line of descendants and relationship each time, though there was no exact moment of dissolution which could be pinpointed, it depending on how long the energy took to level out. Hence the girl retained her clothes for quite a while before they disappeared. I understand that Guard Sixty-Seven tried to give you the girl's clothes and found they had gone. Since he hadn't noticed their disappearance — or rather detected a decrease in the weight of the bag — it is possible that they vanished at the very moment he tried to produce them.

'Even silkworms vanished,' Clem finished. 'They were the remote 'descendants' of the silkworms which had created the silk for the girl's dress. Entropy caught up, right through the line again, evolved them over a thousand years and they consequently vanished. Consider the untold millions of silkworms which must have evolved in the interval, from the original progenitors, and it will be seen that very few silkworms could escape being involved, which is why all of them vanished on the transatlantic ship. Let us hope that the entropy balance will soon be reached and the disasters besetting us will cease.'

The Master was silent for nearly three minutes when Clem had finished speaking, so much so it appeared that he had gone to sleep. Apparently such was not the case for at last he stirred. 'I accept the explanation, Mister Bradley,' he said. 'I have been deliberating the various scientific issues and I see nothing which is at variance with logic — at least as far as the various articles connected with this woman are concerned. As you say, let us hope that the energy will soon find its level and that our troubles may cease. I think, however, that you neglected a factor in your otherwise excellent hypothesis.'

'And what is that, sir?'

'What of the woman herself? Why has not entropy caught up with her? Since the various articles and garments connected with her have disappeared, and their entropy been transmitted down a direct descending line, is it not possible that this woman, too, will be involved?'

'That,' Clem admitted, 'is a thought which has worried me quite a deal, sir, but so far nothing has happened to her.'

'That does not imply that it will do so later. Her energy must have been given off and transmitted through — 'The Master sat up abruptly. 'Had she any descendants? Progeny?' he asked, his eyes sharpening.

'A son, sir.' Clem's expression changed too as he suddenly realized the implications. 'Great heavens! The deaths of cattle have proven that entropy reacts through organic bodies as it does through inorganic substances. That means that all those connected with her, in a descending line, will find entropy catching up on them!'

'Yes. And she herself will vanish,' the Master added. 'She must, because, by the law of entropy, she is nearly a thousand years old! My conception of the problem is that so far this woman's entropy has not found its level, therefore none of her descendants has been affected, or she either. But once the level is found . . .'

Silence dropped, and Clem and Buck exchanged glances of dismay.

'It also depends,' the Master continued, 'on whether or not her son married and had issue — and on whether they in turn also married. So far nothing has happened since no mysterious deaths have been reported anywhere. I think we cannot do better than look through the records and see if we can trace this woman and her family. Her name is — what?'

'Lucy Denby,' Clem answered, thinking, 'and she was married round about 2007 to a Reginald Denby, salesman, or something.'

'I will see what I can trace.'

Obviously disturbed by this new possibility the Master reached out to a switch, and then he paused, looking at his hand. Normally it was tanned and thin, but now it was a deathly white with the veins etched in a vivid blue tracery. He looked at his other hand sharply and found it similarly afflicted.

'Strange,' he murmured, preoccupied with this metamorphosis. 'Very strange.'

Buck gripped Clem's arm tightly, but Clem had no need of this to apprehend the sudden change that had come over the Master. His face was dissolving into a mass of seams and lines. He seemed now to be unable to move, held in the grip of the astounding metabolism suddenly coursing through him. Heat was spreading from him as his life-energy took a mighty surge forward. With the passing seconds his iron-gray hair became white: then he was bald!

'Great cosmos,' Buck whispered, transfixed.

'Must — trace — records — ' the Master whispered; then his face caved in and his hands shrank to bony claws. He spoke no more words, but the look in his dying eyes was of one who tries to understand and cannot. They dimmed to burned-out coals. His skinny, fleshless frame flopped to the desk. Nor did it stay there. Vast age crumbled his bones to dust and an empty suit of clothes dropped to the floor.

'He's — gone,' Clem gulped, his jaw lolling in stupour.

Buck could not find any words for the moment — then the private loudspeaker on the late Master's desk suddenly burst into life.

'Emergency Communication to the Master! An unexpected wave of senility is sweeping the world! Particularly severe within a hundred miles' radius. Isolated instances in remoter areas. Please advise.'

Clem jumped up, then in a passable imitation of the Master's voice he said briefly: 'Later!' Switching off again he turned a scared face to Buck.

'Naturally you've grasped what's happened?' he asked. 'Presumably the very thing the Master was discussing has happened! Lucy's entropy is beginning to work through her line of descendants. We certainly don't need to hunt through the records to see if her son married and had children. The Master must have been a descendant, too, however remotely. Come to think of it, in a thousand years, the descendants of one person might run into tens of thousands — '

'No might about it,' Clem snapped. 'The fact that people in all walks of life have suddenly started dying is proof of it. What's worrying me is whether we'll find Lucy herself alive any more! Maybe she's vanished like the things she was wearing.'

'To me there's a bigger worry,' Buck retorted. 'How do we explain the disappearance of the Master? We are known to be the last people to see him alive — the guard will verify that — and I'm getting cold all over thinking what the law will do when it investigates.'

Clem got to his feet and looked at the clothes on the floor.

'For the moment,' he said, 'those clothes will, I hope baffle those who find them. Our only chance is to walk out of here as though nothing had happened and get back quick to the underground where we'll think up what comes next. Come on.'

6

The past is present

To get safely out of the official building was not particularly difficult since it was assumed by the guards, number Sixty-Seven amongst them, that the Master had released Clem and Buck from audience and allowed them to go on their way, and they reached the underground workings safely and, to Clem's intense relief, Lucy was still where she had been left, high up amidst the rockery and effectively screened. She listened in silent amazement to the story Clem had to tell.

'Then what happens now?' she asked anxiously.

'I don't dare to think,' Clem groaned. 'Once the disappearance of the Master is discovered trouble is going to come our way with a capital T. That guard, number Sixty-Seven, is a particularly vindictive specimen who'll shift heaven and earth to make capital out of this.'

'It all seems so queer,' Lucy mused. 'That so many people are dying because of me. Even queerer that the Master of this amazing world should be a descendant of mine! I don't know whether to feel proud or — or revolted! Queer too that steel and all the rest of it should be wiped out in so many places because I happened to be wearing them at the time. Why don't I disappear then? I should, surely, if everything is to hang together?'

'That is a possibility even yet,' Clem said quietly, and searched her face. He read no fear there: only that same look of bewilderment that had been hers ever since the rescue from the entropy globe.

'Well, if it comes to it,' she said seriously, 'I shan't even have the chance to thank you for all you've done — you and Buck and Eva, so I'll thank you now, just in case. I also apologize most sincerely for having thrown a good-sized spanner into the works of 3004.'

Clem gave a fleeting smile as he patted her hand, and then he became serious again. 'I only hope this entropy business doesn't work out to its logical conclusion in your case, Lucy, because I've more than a liking for you — as you may have noticed.'

'I've noticed,' she assented, smiling. 'But you've forgotten, surely, that I'm a misfit? The odd girl out? And, anyway, I'm a thousand years behind the times.'

'That doesn't signify to me. What I want to do, if some scientific miracle spares your dissolution, is to prove to the world what I proved to the Master — that you are a helpless victim in need of assistance and not condemnation. I did prove it to him, and he accepted the theory. Then he had to die before he could speak! It's damnable. It puts us right back where we started, but with the added burden of knowing that the Master is dead — '

'Hey, listen to that radio,' Buck interrupted, making his way amidst the rockery. 'If it doesn't smell like trouble I don't know what does!'

Clem and the girl listened, and so did the working crew in the great open space below. The words from the speaker came through with a powerful echo.

'Attention all listeners! The Master has disappeared! No trace of him can be found, and the only clue is his clothes on the floor of his office, obviously left there by his abductors. We need no further proof that spies are at work and this is their supreme and most audacious move. War with the East is imminent, according to private papers, which the Master had in his possession — so imminent indeed that Leslie Hurst, our ambassador, is already on his way home. The move of abducting the Master is plain. Without him, and his guiding genius we cannot possibly survive in the struggle with the East that is to come!

'Attention all listeners! To round up every spy in the Western organization here in the West is obviously impossible. We have already tried and made little headway — but it is known that one of these spies is being shielded by Clement Bradley and his partner 'Buck' Cardew at the foundation site of the Protection Tower — which Tower, incidentally, should have been erected by now if it is to be of service in defeating invaders. The delay in constructing the foundations is now shown as obviously intentional. Further — a vital fact — it is known that the two last people to be present with the Master before his mysterious disappearance were Bradley and Cardew. Find them at the Protection Tower site — and find the woman with them — then we shall have the answer to many of our problems. One hostage, in the form of this woman, may do much to deter Eastern onslaught. All of you, men and women, wherever you may be, have freedom to act as you see fit in bringing these traitors to account.'

'I wouldn't be sure of it,' Buck said, 'but that sounded like the voice of Guard Sixty-Seven, taking a great deal of authority unto himself!'

'It was Sixty-Seven,' Clem confirmed. 'As for him taking authority unto himself, he wouldn't dare without the sanction of the Council over which the Master ruled. The only explanation is that he must have told them he has special knowledge regarding us, so they've put him in charge of the situation for the moment. Far as we're concerned, the people will be out to get us — particularly as the news of imminent war has now been broken.'

'We'll fight it out,' Buck decided. He got to his feet and called to the assembly of men gathered in the space below. 'Hey, boys! You heard that broadcast? You willing to fight it out against the mob?'

The steel-helmeted heads nodded and one of them called back: 'Sure thing, Buck! We'll give them a run for their money if they come down here!'

'All right then — scatter to convenient positions and use the blast-guns as weapons,' Buck ordered. 'That ought to let 'em see we mean business.'

'I think this is a waste of time,' Clem said frankly. 'I know the blast-guns can wreak a tremendous amount of havoc — massacre if you like — but it won't stop a determined people who think we've sold them into defeat against the East. If anything it'll only make our case all the blacker because it will look as though we really are guilty if we try and defend ourselves.'

'That's right,' Lucy assented, clinging to Clem's arm. 'Honest, Buck, I think Clem's got the right idea.'

'Then you're both crazy!' Buck snorted. 'If you're both so chicken-hearted that you intend to let yourselves be taken without a struggle, I'm not. Don't you realize what it will mean when the mob gets you? Law will be thrown overboard. Many will revert to type and maybe you'll even be lynched. In fact, if Sixty-Seven is controlling things for the moment I'm more than sure you will be!'

'No.' Clem shook his head. 'Even Sixty-Seven would not dare go that far: the Council would prevent it. My idea is to let ourselves be taken and then prove the truth of what did happen to the Master, and his acceptance of my theory concerning Lucy.'

'Oh, talk sense, can't you!' Buck cried. 'We can never prove what happened in that office — '

'Yes we can,' Clem interrupted. 'Providing it's still there, that is, and I'm hoping it will be. Don't you remember that when our interview with the Master began he switched on a recording apparatus so our entire conversation could be taken down. When I'd finished he switched it off.'

'Yes, that's true, but — ' Buck scratched his neck. 'But that doesn't explain the Master's disappearance!'

'It would to the more intelligent members of the Council, because the Master himself put forward the theory that any descendants of Lucy might be affected. The Council will couple together the disappearance of the Master with the other cases of senility sweeping the world and that will clear things up. Finally, the Master's acceptance of Lucy as a woman of a thousand years ago will be taken as correct for it has always been said that the Master was never wrong in a scientific verdict.'

'It's a chance, of course,' Buck admitted, 'but I'd much prefer some kind of tangible action, instead of just pinning our hopes on a possibility like that. Seems too flimsy a thing to hope for, and if Sixty-Seven has destroyed that spoken record, what then? He had obviously been examining the Master's papers and — '

'He wouldn't,' Clem interrupted. 'Damn it, man, Sixty-Seven is only an officer guard: he wouldn't dare probe that much. It would be the officiating members of the Council who'd do that, and I'm hoping that they didn't think of starting up the recording machine. Or on the other hand, if they did — or do — our problem may be solved for us.'

Buck, clearly, was still not completely convinced, but before he could pursue the argument any further there came the gathering sound of voices in the underworld and the noise of advancing feet. Down below, the grimy, set-faced engineering crew maneuvered the powerful blast-guns into prearranged positions and crouched before the sights watching for the first appearance of the invaders.

Suddenly the first hastily armed civilians appeared and at the same moment Buck let out a mighty yell.

'Hold your fire, boys! Hold it!'

Men and women, in twos and threes

and then in groups, followed by armed members of the police, came drifting down into the workings. There seemed to be no end to them as they congregated, filling up the tunnels that led into the great space.

Then, from amongst them, Sixty-Seven became visible. He had his gun in his hand and appeared almost disappointed that he had no occasion to use it.

'Better come down from there, Bradley!' he called. 'You too, Cardew; and that woman you've got with you. Glad you know when you're beaten.'

'Don't think you're standing there untouched because I want it!' Buck shouted. 'If I'd have had my way you'd be blasted to powder by now — but my partner here is more sentimental, or crazy. I haven't decided which.'

'Come down!' Sixty-Seven ordered. 'And hurry it up.'

There was nothing else for it. Buck led the way down the rocky slope from the high niche, and Clem came after him, holding on to Lucy's arm. Sixty-Seven eyed her fixedly as she came forward.

'Chief spy for the Easterners, eh?' he asked dryly. 'I've been quite a while catching up on you, young woman, but I'll make up for lost time now I've started. I don't suppose there can be a lower form of life than a dirty female spy who sells herself to the East — '

Sixty-Seven did not get any further. Buck lashed out with all the power of his massive right arm. The iron knuckles struck the guard clean in the mouth, splitting his lip and spinning him back against the rocks.

'Good,' Buck grinned, palming his throbbing knuckles. 'Now I feel better! Shoot me down if you like and I'll die happy.'

Probably his suggestion would have been adopted had Sixty-Seven been alone — but he was not, and even he realized that ruthless shooting amongst so many witnesses would not stand him in very good stead as an officer of the law.

'All right,' he said thickly, straightening up and dabbing at his bleeding mouth. 'I'll not forget that, Cardew! That's the second time you've hit me in the course of my duty and I'll see the Council hears of it! Now get on your way, all three of you. You've a lot to explain.'

In a close-knit trio the three started walking, followed and partly surrounded by the mob. The engineers were left behind since there was no legal claim against them. So at length the journey through the tunnels was ended and the march to the city center began. There was no other way of covering the distance since so many people made vehicular transportation impossible.

Then gradually it dawned on Clem at least that the route was not leading towards the great building where stood the headquarters of the Council and, at its summit, the office of the late Master. Instead the mob was moving in the direction of one of the biggest public lecture halls.

'What's the idea?' Clem asked Sixty-Seven sharply, as he paced along, smothering his bleeding mouth. 'Where are we going?'

'The City Hall, where proper justice

can be meted out,' came the muffled response. 'This isn't a matter for the Council to decide, Bradley: it's up to the people. They are the ones who have been betrayed, not the Council.'

'As a citizen I demand the Council chamber!' Clem cried in fury. 'You can't take the law into your own hands like this!'

'I'm not doing it. I'm obeying the orders of the people because I'm a public servant. If you don't like it complain to the people who now have you in their midst.'

Clem looked about him but he said nothing. It was possible that Sixty-Seven was correct, and that he dare not cross the will of the incensed multitude. Whatever the answer the journey ended within the mighty City Hall, which was already packed to capacity. And the capture of the trio had evidently been considered a foregone conclusion for on the rostrum usually reserved for lecturers there now sat three men. Clem and Buck both recognized them as they were bundled along with Lucy in their midst.

They were the three whose finances helped to build the city's prosperity — not members of the Governing Council as such, but certainly capable of wielding a tremendous influence in public affairs.

Chairs had been roughly placed to form a 'dock' for the three prisoners and here they were directed and then left. For a long time there was the shuffle of feet and scraping of chairs as guards and public alike took their seats, the overflow of men and women straining at the doors.

'Doesn't look too damned healthy for the recorder in the Master's office,' Buck murmured bitterly, as Clem stood beside him. 'You'd have done better to let me have my way. At least we'd have blasted about three-hundred out of existence and that would have been something.'

'It would only have condemned us all the more,' Clem muttered. 'Don't be so infernally violent in your aims!'

'In this court,' declared the centermost man suddenly, 'there will be no attempt to follow the pedantry of the law because we are not a legally constituted body. We are a court of the people, convened by the people, and the decision we reach shall be that of the people.'

'If this is not a legally constituted court you have no legal right to try us,' Clem retorted. 'As a citizen I therefore demand liberty — or, failing that, a proper hearing before the Council.'

'The Council is not concerned with this matter,' the impromptu 'judge' answered. 'It is so long since a crime of any importance happened that normal courts do not exist any more — as you should know. Hence this hastily-devised one to try you three on the serious charge of international sabotage and abduction of the Master of the West!'

'And if you arrive at the decision that we are guilty, who is going to pronounce sentence?' Clem asked. 'None of you has the right to do it.'

'It is not a question of having the right, Mister Bradley. The issue is up to the people. To the most vital point first: where is the Master?'

'Dead — of old age,' Clem snapped.

A murmur went through the people

and the three men on the rostrum looked at each other questioningly; then the centermost turned to face Clem again.

'I hope, Mister Bradley, you are not going to be so foolish as to use the present all-prevailing senility as an excuse for your behavior? The Master couldn't have died of old age. Such a thing is not even possible. He has been hidden somewhere, was probably removed under heavy disguise which accounts for his clothes being left behind.'

Clem breathed hard. 'If I were to explain this matter in full detail I would only be derided by you and the people, because it involves a most complicated scientific theory — but the Master understood it, and accepted it. Will you be content to base your decision on the Master's own conclusions?'

'So you mean to restore him from — wherever you have hidden him?'

'Nothing of the kind. The Master is extinct, dying of age so great that even his body turned to dust. However, he recorded the interview Mister Cardew and I had with him, and to the best of my knowledge that recording is still in his office if I could be allowed to obtain it.'

'That's only fair, surely?' Buck demanded.

'You have overlooked the fact that you are prisoners,' the 'judge' snapped, 'and such a request as you have made cannot be granted. In any case we have no guarantee that the recording to which you refer would prove genuine. Since the abduction of the Master must obviously have been planned in detail long ago, there would be nothing to prevent scientists faking a recording purporting to belong to the Master. Nothing would be easier than to leave it in his office at the time of the abduction, to be used later as so-called proof of innocence. I, and the people, can well understand how essential it is that you three should escape justice since you are obviously the cleverest spies in the entire Eastern organization — '

'We've nothing to do with the Eastern organization!' Buck roared in fury. 'Why can't you three men up there use some commonsense? Any man, or woman, no matter what their crime, is entitled to use every available form of evidence to prove innocence. That's all we're asking for.'

'And it is not granted!' the 'judge' retorted.

'Who says it isn't?' a voice asked coldly — and immediately attention was distracted from the 'judge' to a man at the back of the hall. Somehow he had reached one of the higher windows and evidently entered thereby. At the moment he stood against the empty top balcony, using its ledge upon which to rest the heavy barrel of a blast-gun. His steel helmet and grimy face immediately betrayed where he had come from.

'The boys!' Buck cried in delight, glancing about him to behold other engineers from the foundation site at different parts of the balcony, their blast-guns poised. 'They've followed us up.'

'That's right, Buck,' agreed the one who had first spoken. 'Since you'd been taken away by the people we decided to see that the people gave you a fair deal

— and at the moment they don't seem to be doing so — '

'Get those men from that balcony!' the 'judge' shouted in fury. 'Whose negligence allowed them to get in, anyway?'

'Not a matter of negligence,' responded the spokesman engineer. 'Everybody's so confoundedly busy trying to crush into this place that nobody's about in the city — and certainly nobody was guarding this building. We just went round the back of it and climbed up to the first story. Now — how about letting the three prisoners have a fair hearing?'

'Waste of time,' Clem called. 'Even if the record was produced they'd say it was faked.'

The engineer considered, his sharp eyes glancing to his comrades at the ready along the balcony, their guns aimed.

'All right,' he said. 'In that case you'd better go — whilst you're safe. We'll cover you.'

The people jumped to their feet in fury, then they hesitated as Clem spoke to them.

'Better look at this thing sensibly,' he

warned. 'I invented the blast-guns these engineers are using and I warn you their power is sufficient to mow down everybody in this hall. Better give us a safe passage if you wish to stay in one piece.'

'And where do we go?' Buck murmured.

'To the Master's office,' Clem whispered. 'The highest point in the city and easy to defend against most comers. Right, let's risk it.'

'I'm going to let the boys know where we're going,' Buck said. 'They can be of tremendous help to us with those blast guns — Follow us to the Master's office, boys!' he yelled, and then hurried after Clem and Lucy as they got on the move.

Under the circumstances there was nothing the people could do with the deadly blast-guns threatening them. Even without the warning Clem had given them they knew the power of the guns because the news announcements had been full of the details at the time Clem had secured his Government contract.

'You can't possibly get away with this!' Guard Sixty-Seven shouted angrily. 'Even less so since you've told us where you're going! What are you people scared of?' he demanded, wheeling round. 'Don't you realize they're getting away? Those men with the blast-guns can't get all of us! Come on!'

Pretty well sure of his safety because he was so hemmed in by the people around him Sixty-Seven plunged in the wake of the departing trio and, moved by his example, the people also started to push and shove. The spokesman-engineer watched the proceedings for a moment, his keen eyes to the sights of his blast-gun.

'I never did like that guard,' he muttered. 'Too much to say for himself — '

Abruptly the guard became visible in the sight for a second or so and the engineer instantly pressed the button. A shaft of violet flame stabbed down from the balcony and struck Sixty-Seven straight in the back. He howled in sudden anguish and then dropped flat on his face, the people around him recoiling hastily and staring over their shoulders, upwards to where the engineer stood.

'Just to warn you,' he shouted. 'If you dare follow those three you know what you'll get! Now get back before I give the order for every gun to be used.'

By this time Clem, Buck and Lucy had reached the main doorway at a slithering run. They glanced back quickly over their shoulders.

'The boys are pinning 'em,' Buck exulted. 'Quick! With things like this we may just make it to the Master's office, and if we get that far there's no reason why we shouldn't be able to get the Council to listen to us later. If they won't listen, then we'll barricade ourselves in until they do.'

'And use what for food?' Clem questioned. 'Anyway, we'll sort that out later — ready for a sprint, Lucy? Here we go.'

Helping the girl between them they hurried out into the main street and, as the engineer had said, it was almost empty of people, most of them having congregated in the vast public hall. What few there were glanced after the scurrying trio but paid no more attention — and since the guards within the public hall were unable to send advance warning to the main headquarters building there was no danger in this direction at the moment, either.

'We'd better take the back entrance and use the service lift,' Clem said quickly, when at last they had reached the broad avenue leading to the rear of the vast building. 'We're not so liable to be questioned.'

Buck nodded, not letting up for a moment in his run. The main doorway to the rear was gained and so was the lift marked STAFF ONLY, which at this period was empty.

'Done it,' Clem panted, slamming across the grille and pushing in the button. 'We'll think out later what we do next.'

To Lucy the journey to the top of the vast edifice seemed interminable and every moment she was expecting the lift to stop, halted by some official order or other, but nothing happened — and at last there was a click as the ascent finished and the lift gates automatically opened on to an opulent corridor. Here indeed were the sacrosanct regions of the building, as Clem and Buck well knew — the private chambers and office of the departed Master.

'There's a guard at the Master's office door,' Lucy whispered, peering outside.

'There is?' Buck clenched his fists. 'I'll deal with him. Follow me.'

Unarmed as he was, and knowing there was no retreat now they had come thus far, he stepped out boldly and advanced. The guard instantly leveled his atom-gun.

'Business?' he asked curtly.

'Urgent,' Buck replied, still on the move. 'You'd better see these papers. There are some records in the Master's office that I have permission to get. See — '

He fumbled in his overalls and unconsciously the guard watched the moving hand. The next thing he knew was that the other hand, bunched into a fist, had lashed a smashing left-hook under his chin. He gulped and his head snapped back to a sharp angle. Before he could attempt to recover the right hand whipped upwards and then descended in a fist on the back of his neck. He flattened knocked out.

'Okay,' Buck called, heaving the unconscious man to one side. 'Coast's clear for the moment.'

Still hanging on to Lucy, Clem hurried forward; then Buck swore under his breath as he tried the Master's office door. It was locked, and made of solid metal so no shoulder heaving could possibly break it open.

'Only one answer,' Buck said, and from the floor he picked up the atom-gun that the guard had dropped.

'That's going to ruin the lock when we want to barricade ourselves in,' Clem pointed out.

'Maybe so, but it's a better alternative than being shut out here, isn't it? The mob'll be after us the moment they dare to risk it.'

He fired the gun into the lock and the third shaft of intolerably bright energy did the trick. Clem hurtled straight into the office and brought up sharp against the desk. Instantly Buck and the girl followed him, then Buck closed the door and used the atom-gun again to fuse frame and door into one solid piece down the opening side.

'May hold,' he said, 'We'll live in hope! Our best place at the moment seems to be the window. We can watch what's happening.'

They moved to it, and for Lucy at least, it was a dizzying experience to gaze down into that two-thousand-foot canyon, of steel and stone and see the main street below like a ribbon amidst the smaller buildings.

'There they come!' Buck exclaimed suddenly, pointing to the left. 'Swarms of 'em! Like ants on a strip of tape.'

His simile was very accurate. In silence Lucy and Clem watched the hordes swelling along the white roadway, plainly heading in the direction of this headquarters building. At this great height, and with the windows closed, there were no sounds, but presumably the mob was shouting for vengeance if their wild, surging movements were any guide.

'I'd give anything at this moment for a stack of bombs,' Buck muttered, glancing angrily around him.

Clem shrugged. 'And what good would that do?'

'Good? Probably save us. I've no illusions about being able to stick in this office indefinitely.'

'Neither have I,' Clem answered. 'Which means we might as well do what we can whilst we are here. Where's that recording machine?'

He hurried across to the desk and looked at the recording instrument. A full reel of tape was on the take-up spool and, as far as could be judged, was the one that had recorded the interview with the Master. Quickly Clem set the machine in reverse until the tape was back at its starting point. A preliminary test satisfied him that it was the interview.

'And how far does that get us?' Buck asked, watching. 'Nobody here to listen except us. It's the people who ought to hear it. Some of them might believe it. However, it can't be done until they break in here, and by that time I fancy they'll be too fighting mad to listen to anything!'

'They can hear it before they break in here,' Clem replied tersely, studying the various instruments on the huge desk. 'Here's a direct transmission radio, used only by the Master, I suppose, but according to the meter readings it is tuned to all public speakers — Yes, that ought to do it, providing the power is permanently on.'

He switched on the apparatus, then when the pilot-light glowed he spoke into the microphone. Apparently nothing happened.

'Can't tell whether this works or not,' he said quickly, glancing up. 'Buck, open the ventilator shaft at the top of the window there: it will enable me to hear my voice in the city if the speakers are working.'

Buck promptly obeyed, studying the still surging mob as he did so. The moment the ventilator opened the noise of the people floated up in an indistin-guishable blur of sound, but a second or two later it was completely swamped by Clem's own vastly amplified voice thun-dering through the public loudspeakers.

'Attention all listeners! Attention to a special broadcast on the wavelength of the late Master!'

'Keep it up!' Lucy exclaimed excitedly, peering below. 'The mob's halted and is listening for what comes next.'

Clem switched on the recorder and the playback voices spoke into the microphone and thence relayed themselves to every public loudspeaker in the city and surrounding districts. Little by little the entire interview with the Master was given, ending at the point where he had decided he must search the records.

'There it is!' Clem cried. 'Believe it or otherwise, but that is a genuine record of what happened. Surely now you can see that the Master was not abducted or murdered? He died as I told you — of extreme old age!'

Clem ceased announcing and hurried to the window to join Buck and the girl in watching the scene below. From the look of things the people were discussing amongst themselves what they should do next — then the attention of the trio was suddenly diverted by the sight of heli-jet 'planes hurtling towards the headquarters building. Apparently they had come from the space-airport a quarter of a mile distant.

'Now what?' Buck looked above, his eyes narrowed. 'Are these devils trying to get at us from the sky as well as the ground?'

'No idea,' Clem muttered, 'but they're certainly headed this way.'

Anxiously he, Buck and Lucy watched. The jet 'planes circled for a few moments, then they made a swift dive to the roof of the headquarters building and landed on the immense flat space. Presumably they did so, at least. From their angle at the window the trio could no longer detect what had happened.

'They're coming on again below,' Lucy said, her voice dispirited. 'Evidently they don't believe what you told them Clem — '

She broke off at a sudden battering din upon the office door.

'Those from the jet 'planes,' Buck snapped. 'A quicker way than coming by the lift. It'll take ages for the mob to get up here anyway — You're wasting your time!' he yelled, as the hammering on the door continued. 'We're not coming out and the door's sealed.'

'It's me, Buck!' a voice shouted. 'Get the door open, can't you? We can't leave you in there — '

'The boys!' Buck gasped, surprised. 'I'd forgotten all about them — Blast the door open if you've got your blast-guns!' he shouted. 'We'll stand clear.'

There was an interval of a moment or two, then a burning redness appeared in the center of the metal door. It quickly changed to white and at last the metal itself began to run like melting butter before the terrific heat of the blast-gun the chief engineer was using. The moment a hole large enough had been made he clambered through into the office, avoiding the searingly hot sides of the opening.

'In you come, boys,' he called, and the rest of the men followed him, bringing the heavy blast-guns on their broad shoulders.

'Nice work,' Buck complimented them.

'Even though I don't quite understand what you did.'

'Simple enough, Buck. When we departed from the balcony of the public hall the people were more concerned in finding you than bothering with us — particularly as we had blast-guns with which to protect ourselves — so we carried the stuff unmolested to the airfield and used six heli-jet 'planes. The authorities couldn't stop us. We were in the air before the facts had dawned on them. Seemed to me the only way to get here ahead of the mob, and now we are here,' the engineer finished grimly, 'we'll give them a run for their money the moment they show themselves through that opening.'

'I don't want any massacre,' Clem snapped.

'Maybe not, Clem, but this is out of your hands now,' Buck answered. 'You've given them the record of the interview and it seems pretty clear that they haven't accepted it. They've come into the building and any moment now they'll be on top of us. I'm for fighting them — to the finish. Even if we go down let's thin their numbers in the process.'

'At least let one of them speak, then,' Clem insisted. 'We don't know that they didn't believe what they heard. If they're still after us then let 'em have it, with my blessing.'

'Right!' Buck gave a grim nod and stood beside the chief engineer behind the line of blast-guns that had now been set in position. Lucy moved back also, Clem's arm about her.

So they waited, listening to the growing sound of the mob ascending from the depths. They were coming by the moving stairways and had evidently swept all opposition out of the way in the process for, normally, nobody could get past the guards in the main hall of the building.

Nearer and nearer still, until their voices began to take on distinctness and their feet made a muffled thunder. And at last the first man and woman appeared — and stopped dead at the sight of the trained blast-guns.

'One step,' Buck warned, 'and it's the

finish! If you're resolved to take us to your blasted people's justice you're going to lose an awful lot of your numbers doing it!'

More men and women piled up behind the two hesitating in the broken doorway, until at last the space was jammed and there were shouts in the corridor demanding to know what was causing the hold-up.

'You heard my broadcast,' Clem snapped. 'What more do you want?'

'We don't believe a word of that rubbish!' one of the men shouted. 'The whole thing was faked to sound like an interview with the Master — just as we were warned it would. You're spies, all three of you, and you've brought about just the chaos you wanted! The whole city full of people out chasing you when we ought to be looking to our defences. Everybody knows by now that at any moment an Eastern armada might be sighted.'

'Hardly so soon,' Clem corrected. 'Ambassador Hurst has not yet returned, and the attack is not likely to start until he has done so. There are rules, even in war.'

'What's all the delay about?' bawled somebody, invisible to those inside the office. 'Go in and get 'em.'

'That's right! Wipe 'em out! They've done their best to ruin the city and — '

'Oh, stop talking like a lot of fools!' Clem cried, incensed. 'You don't seriously believe that any agents, no matter how capable, could bring about the death of people from old age in widely differing parts of the world, do you? The whole thing is explained by released entropy, entropy chained down for a thousand years by an unusually clever scientist. The Master believed it, and so must you — '

He broke off for the sudden surging of the people to the rear of those in the broken doorway forced those almost within the office to tumble inside it. Buck half raised his arm to give the signal to fire, but when it came to it even he could not give the okay to a massacre, which it certainly would have been had the blast-guns opened up. A second later he regretted it for, seizing their chance, the

178

mob rolled in irresistibly, surrounding the guns and the trio who now stood together.

The man who had appointed himself the spokesman of the mob came forward, a sour grin of triumph on his face.

'This time there won't be any mistakes,' he said. 'Not even a trial for we're convinced it isn't necessary anymore. When the partial wrecking of a city and the killing off of its people — to say nothing of cattle — is put down to entropy being tied up for a thousand years you stand condemned by your own audacity. Unfortunately the Council won't let us use the lethal chamber: in fact they won't let us do anything without a trial. So we'll act on our own. Members of the Council did their best to stop us getting into this building — but most of 'em won't do it again. All right, tie 'em up,' he ordered.

There was nothing the three could do, pinioned on all sides. Thin cabling was ruthlessly ripped from the instruments on the Master's desk and used to bind the wrists and ankles of the three tightly.

'Why all this preliminary?' Clem asked bitterly. 'There are blast-guns there. Why don't you use them and get it over with?'

'Bit too effective,' the spokesman answered. 'Like using a cannon to swat a fly. Besides, some of us might get hurt, too. No, there's a better way. We're two-thousand feet up here. Do I have to say more? Start moving to that window!'

'What?' Lucy gasped in horror. 'You don't mean that you're going to — '

'We mean that you're going to go down a lot quicker than you came up. Drastic but necessary. In fact much too good for three spies who — ' The spokesman broke off and turned, frowning, at interruptions from the corridor. A second or two later the reason became obvious as a strongly-built immaculately-dressed man, carrying a bulging briefcase in his hand, stepped through the broken door.

'Leslie. Hurst!' Clem cried thankfully, recognizing the famous ambassador. 'Oh, thank God you came at this moment, Mister Hurst! These people will not believe — '

'These people,' Hurst said, with a cold

glance around him, 'are behaving like a lot of recessive units. Every one of you ought to be ashamed of yourselves!' he went on angrily. 'What's the use of a scientific upbringing if you don't use it? Cut those three free instantly.'

Such was his air of command he was obeyed, though reluctantly and the people stood looking at him grimly. It was only his unexpected arrival and apparent complete lack of fear that had enabled him to stride into their midst in any case.

'For your edification,' he said, 'I heard over my personal radio, which is tuned to the Master's private waveband, all that was going on in here. When you gave your original announcement concerning the interview you had with the Master, Mister Bradley, you evidently didn't switch off afterwards. I gathered exactly what was happening and came on the last lap of my journey with all speed. I would have been here some days ago except for an important happening in the Eastern hemisphere.'

Everybody waited, then Hurst finished: 'You idiots who were so determined to kill this young woman, along with Mister Bradley and Mister Cardew here, ought to go down on your knees to her in thankfulness. Because of her, because of the fact that she lived a thousand years ago and revived again in this age, the threat of war has been destroyed. If that doesn't prove she isn't a spy I don't know what does.'

'But — but how do you mean?' Lucy herself asked blankly.

'I mean,' Hurst replied deliberately, 'that Generals Zoam and Niol, who were directly responsible for wanting war with the West, have both died of extreme senility. President Ilof radioed the news to me when I was on my return flight, so I went back. I found, as I have always believed, that president Ilof is a peace-loving man and desires nothing more than friendly relations between the hemispheres. Apart from Generals Niol, and Zoam, hundreds of other people in the Eastern hemisphere have died too. The reason? This woman here! Zoam and Niol, like many Easterners, were also remote descendants of Lucy Denby. That fact has saved all of us, and re-established relations between the two hemispheres on a better footing than ever . . . As for our own Master, it is for the Council to decide who must succeed him.'

'Then — then that interview was true?' gasped the spokesman for the people.

'Every word of it, and this girl you have vilified is your savior. Now, apologize, and make a fresh demand — that she be given city status.'

The people turned from Hurst to look at the girl. So did Clem and Buck. Then they were silent, stunned by the unbelievable as the last piece in the puzzle had evidently resolved itself.

Lucy Denby had vanished — but her clothes remained.

THE END

We do hope that you have enjoyed reading this large print book.

Did you know that all of our titles are available for purchase?

We publish a wide range of high quality large print books including:
Romances, Mysteries, Classics
General Fiction
Non Fiction and Westerns

Special interest titles available in large print are:
The Little Oxford Dictionary
Music Book, Song Book
Hymn Book, Service Book

Also available from us courtesy of Oxford University Press:
Young Readers' Dictionary
(large print edition)
Young Readers' Thesaurus
(large print edition)

For further information or a free brochure, please contact us at:
Ulverscroft Large Print Books L
The Green, Bradgate Road, Anst
Leicester, LE7 7FU, England.
Tel: (00 44) 0116 236 4325
Fax: (00 44) 0116 234 0205

CLIMATE INCORPORATED
THE FIVE MATCHBOXES
EXCEPT FOR ONE THING
BLACK MARIA, M.A.
ONE STEP TOO FAR
THE THIRTY-FIRST OF JUNE
THE FROZEN LIMIT
ONE REMAINED SEATED
THE MURDERED SCHOOLGIRL
SECRET OF THE RING
OTHER EYES WATCHING
I SPY . . .
FOOL'S PARADISE
DON'T TOUCH ME
THE FOURTH DOOR
THE SPIKED BOY
THE SLITHERERS
MAN OF TWO WORLDS
THE ATLANTIC TUNNEL
THE EMPTY COFFINS
LIQUID DEATH
PATTERN OF MURDER
NEBULA
THE LIE DESTROYER